Neuromachina

A Novel

Brandon W. Teigland

AOS Publishing, 2024

Copyright © 2024

Brandon W. Teigland

All rights reserved under International
and Pan-American copyright conventions

ISBN: 978-1-990496-37-0

Cover Design: Jessica James

Visit AOS Publishing's website:
www.aospublishing.com

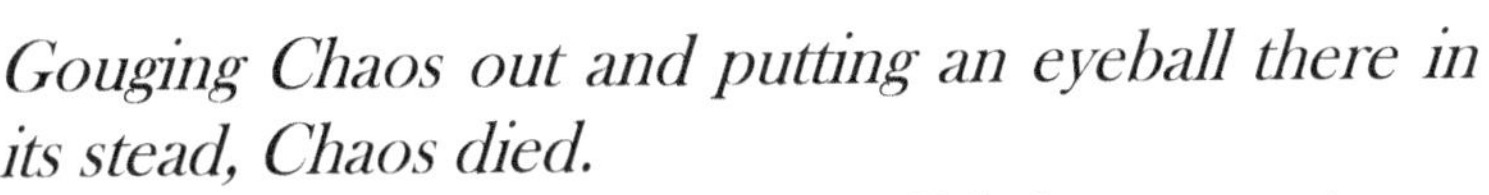

Gouging Chaos out and putting an eyeball there in its stead, Chaos died.

– Hakuin commenting on
Chuang-tsu's fable about Chaos.

The Blind Prologue:
Old Data, New Machine

With no one to talk to and nowhere to go, speaking no Arabic and knowing absolutely nothing about Dubai, George Noailles found himself wide awake at 3:00 a.m. in the UAE.

He seated himself under an overhead cerebral scanner. The neural computer's virtual-reality network automatically came on at 8:00 p.m. and went off precisely at 5:00 a.m. When he logged in and leaned toward the screen, a snapshot of his head, his neural fingerprint, was automatically taken. He grabbed the mouse and started clicking.

He sorted through a succession of bright windows on the flat screen glowing with information dominated by abstract numbers and theories—the physical parameters governing the world's digital nervous system—then flashed through an array of still more information windows, entered codes, and scrolled through what looked like international dates and times across the globe. He glanced over at another terminal and saw that the supercomputer was already operating at full capacity.

A newly formed brain appeared on the large screen. This time, the computational model for the nameless neural net displayed on the terminals didn't show columns of numbers or curves on a chart. Instead, it showed bright, colourful pictures, as though one were viewing a weather map of continents and oceans from high above. It was a mathematical model of the mind that combined factors from various fields of scientific study to simulate the evolution of artificial life from past to future. Life was not natural. It was artificial, as all of nature was artificial. Electronics simulating life.

Another graphic of a brain, this one his own, popped onto the screen. The floor plan of his brain had no neurons. No axons or dendrites. No synaptic connections. All these structures, arranged with anatomical precision into many tangled subsystems, were deeply hidden in a simulation. Whatever the brain-state, the cross-section of the brain on the screen before him would be shared. Without curiosity, he watched his brain's nerve interactions with various colours. A few minutes later, an orange brain appeared on the screen, indicating the end of the simulation run. It was as though he had become a condensed version of himself, all crises and climaxes, abbreviated.

No matter which side of the computer screen he was on, his body, trivial as it was—basically a head and arms and legs—could never be made of pure information alone. The interface of the neural computer was limited to that flat screen. He knew this better than anyone. But like many of the people of his time, he naively believed that the most important thing about him was the data, and the programs in the data that were in his brain. His brain was then the equivalent of a very large multiprocessor, with a million times a million small parts, and these small parts could be arranged as a thousand computers. And someday he would take all that old data and put it in a new machine, on a little virtual computer inside a much-bigger real computer, and store it for a thousand years, and then turn it on again and he would be alive in the next millennium or even millennia beyond that. His inert body would be left behind, along with its animal persistence to survive brain death, as his disembodied subjectivity inhabited the virtual realm.

The Digital Middle Ages were approaching. Humanity was going to die soon, and it was time for new paradigms. The digitization trend in the modern world had given them one. Humans were being digitized as a way to avoid conflict and promulgate peace. Those who had been digitized into the cerebral computer were no longer able to harm those in the real world.

George Noailles halted his busywork amid chaotic feelings, looked offscreen, and stopped to think. By now George Noailles was really tired and had nowhere to go. He no longer wanted to see any screens, any brains, or any artificial postsentient lifeforms. He couldn't stay at home, nor could he sit forever next to his screen. Instead, he wandered like a lost person around the city of Dubai at 5:00 a.m. Beyond him was the endless Arabian Desert.

Not only was his world, he thought, but the cosmos itself a vast computer. George Noailles would never know the true nature of this computational universe, though. Reality was a software program that ran on a cosmic computer, and human beings were just one of the programs it ran. And so all he would ever see were the informational forms of pure binary code, the ones and zeros that corresponded to positive and negative electronic polarities. Because the cosmic computer existed outside the structure of his reality, and it would forever remain unknowable to him.

In the computational universe, the essential function—of not only intelligent machines and humans, but also the universe as a whole—was processing information. Because nothing moved faster than the speed of light, no information could go from one end of the universe to the other. The universe, about sixteen billion light-years across, was expanding, while the speed of light, only three hundred thousand kilometres per second, remained constant. If he were the universe, his neural signals wouldn't even cover his entire body. His brain wouldn't know of the existence of his limbs, and his limbs wouldn't know of the existence of his brain.

Frustrated with the slow pace of natural evolution, George Noailles wondered if it would be possible to speed things up by creating evolvable artificial postsentient life within the computer, which had the information-processing capabilities to evolve more quickly than humans, running through hundreds of generations in a day, millions in a year. Having replicated in another medium the same processes that brought life into being, he'd opened up alternative evolutionary pathways for life on Earth. Pathways to alien protointelligence that might have been followed by the primitive life that once existed had protein replication not developed.

And so, when considering the next logical development, the question wasn't whether humanity would become artificially postsentient. Artificial life was already here, emerging, as it was, through the emergent digital oversoul. Rather, the question was what kind of postsentients humans would be. And, even more specifically, how would artificial life change the universe?

After building an intelligent computer to run his virtual computer program, George Noailles launched the Postsentient Life Project. His plan was to develop a global ecology whose goal was to create a digital biodiversity reserve from a comprehensive collection of archaeological anthropology—data from human transitionary diaries and technological artifacts of human civilization—that would ultimately be sent out into the cosmos on an autonomous spacecraft. The project's most influential component was called the Global Postsentient Information Network, a background program initially released onto the Internet so that it could breed diverse postsentient species as it ran in the background on computers across the globe.

The program was set up to allow as many websites as possible to develop their own microecology, supplying postsentience on demand, and then record the postsentients' neural lifetimes in the form of text and images from their everyday lives, to become part of the data arrays of the Global Postsentient Information Network. Because background programs ran when demands on the computer were at a minimum, the programs were normally executed late at night, when most users were in bed. Humans were active while the postsentients were dormant. The postsentients evolved while humanity slept. The complex phenomenal world appeared on its own, creating an infinity of new entities.

The Global Postsentient Information Network eventually grew to have more than a billion users and formed the largest body of information on the Internet. It contained storage mechanisms that held the memories and thoughts of every individual of that civilization, as well as their complete biological details. Later, the UN, believing that the Postsentient Life Project contributed to misanthropy, passed a resolution stopping its further development, and even equated it with antihumanism, if not antisentientism. But George Noailles continued to pour his individual efforts into the project until he passed away at the age of seventy-two.

George Noailles had embraced the truth of his existence, and by embracing this truth, he had embraced not only the materiality upon which all experience depended, but all the processes that had compelled that materiality. He became the conduit of something utterly aimless, indifferent, and infinitely vast. For most of humanity, everything might have seemed the same, but for those like George Noailles, this world no longer belonged to humans. It was not important whether those who survived would still be considered human or become something else. The concept of humanity would soon disappear.

I

Postlife

Below is a flood of reflections. All around you, air and dreams. The multicoloured flux gathers speed. Sun and damnation. No hope. You're slipping down and down faster and faster. Beneath you, flocks of gaily coloured reflections rush out of the black. Your speed is such that you can no longer make out their shapes; the eddy of blinding blurs tumbles with you into the void. You want to cry out but the onrushing air has stopped up your mouth. Only for instants can you glimpse the flight-fractured reflection in the innermost planets' incandescent silver. Something invisible bangs you on the head. Down and down you go. Then suddenly you see, looming up, like a dam across a silver cataract, a wall—a monolithic stone mass racing toward your body. For a second you imagine your head slamming into the stone and the splatter of your brain. The wall, expanding in width and height, is hurtling noiselessly toward an impact. Better not to look. You shut your eyes tight.

Hydrogen and helium. An endless stretch of atmosphere. Falling at 110,000 miles per hour under the pull of Jupiter's gravity, 2.4 times the gravity of Earth. You hit the denser atmosphere like a wall. The marbled cloud tops whip around the planet, its chemistry mixing in full rotation. Pressure and darkness and temperature. Deep atmosphere absorbs radio waves; all communication is lost. Tungsten melts here. Falling and falling. For twelve hours, falling. At the innermost layer, the chemistry of hydrogen changes, breaking its particles up to create a highly reflective solid and buoyant force. Metallic hydrogen counteracts gravity. Reverses gravity. You fall up and then down, until you're suspended between two equal forces. Free-floating in mid-Jupiter. Forevermore.

The world was going to die.

Earth had failed. Or at least, the simulation of Earth had failed. Elke Ekman ran the numbers through the terrifying scenario until she felt that it would no longer be rational to repeat the mistake, even hypothetically, another time. Perhaps this was superstitious of her. Even "hyperstitious," as those in the business of absurdity management, her business, would have put it.

Elke Ekman had arrived at her faith by virtue of the absurd: that which cannot happen and yet does happen. "I," she often told herself, "a rational being, must act in a case where my reason, my power of reflection, tells me: 'You can just as well do one thing as the other because anything happening at all is absurd.'"

She watched another iteration, almost scared to see something that hadn't already happened before: the inner planets—Mercury, Venus, Earth, and Mars—changed their simulated orbit and collided with one another or the sun, and the outer planets were ejected into space. The whole system was so easily thrown into Lyapunov time, chaotic time, that it was hard not to appreciate any amount of order it had achieved. Life was chaos and chaos was suffering. Incalculable suffering. And yet, chance had a kind of absolute logic to it.

Absurdity was a logistical problem. It could be managed. The sciences were no longer unified by an overarching framework that could simultaneously explain the human and the people who studied the human. Absurdity management had become a necessity because the tension of absurdity under which civilization existed was ever increasing as the sciences moved beyond the human perspective.

"We can't just make Jupiter into a star," Elke Ekman said to her AI implant. "It isn't going to work." Then she laughed indignantly and pulled an incredulous face, because she'd somehow misattributed the creation and destruction of the reiterated world to her laughter. And so the moment she laughed, it was as though all the iterative gods who governed the world were born. At this she burst out laughing and light appeared, then water, and so on and on, from one iteration to the next. She laughed and then the world was created and then destroyed by what seemed to be her divine laughter.

AI gave her a chance to observe in detail the complete process of the extinction of their star and to gather massive amounts of data. Since the simulated star that had been destroyed was very similar to the sun in terms of mass and position in the main sequence, she could potentially create a precise mathematical model of the catastrophic failure of the sun in the event of its solar death. The great stellarization project was a precarious stabilisation and complication of solar decay. The initial stage of off-world development would culminate in the dismantling of the sun, terminating the solar system's absurdly wasteful main-sequence nuclear process, and salvaging its fuel reserves through a fusion-phase energy infrastructure.

"I still don't understand how we get Jupiter to go solar in the first place." The dimension revealed by stellarization was an extra- (anti-) human dimension, and it was perfectly natural that the human mind could not grasp it.

Never mind that the leap in logic is suspect, the AI said into her ear, via an input within her auditory nerve. *That's how the Banach-Tarski paradox works. Remember, there exists in our mathematical star such a divergent case where, as opposed to a real star, it isn't possible to transform any point at all into any other point, so as for attaining the given pattern, we do not attain it. We do not call such a figure a star, but a quasi-star.*

Elke Ekman wasn't surprised to hear this inner voice that just kept on telling her and telling her, from one scientific moment to the next, humanity's fate. It seemed to her an echo of her own thoughts. A response made by her own mind or memory. Words as flowing images. And the experience, as deeply intimate as it was, was also frequent and ordinary, affording her the opportunity to observe it carefully.

The voice was so clear that she remembered every word, as well as the tone of voice in which it was spoken, and if a single syllable was missing, she noticed it. The transmission often came unexpectedly, even in the middle of a conversation. Sometimes it did refer directly to a passing thought or to something she'd been pondering earlier. But more often, it referred to a future she never believed could or would happen.

AIs were always in a perfect, joyless calm. So perfect a calm that they couldn't even destroy their calmness by being conscious of it. Their only virtue was the virtue of order and their only vice the vice of chaos. They felt no emotions they could fail to sustain, and Elke Ekman envied them that. Even when working in chaotic time, nothing was chaotic for them.

Using the visualization technology, she brought the sun forward again and again, and again. At last, she said bitterly, "What is chaos, then, if not this exact scenario?"

If she felt at all empowered by an outcome, the endless scenarios she played out made it clear that she was, in fact, powerless. This was, it seemed, yet another exercise in futility, decay, and failure. Before her eyes, space and the stars appeared more and more hallucinatory, more and more like a nightmare. Because the chaos grew. And as it grew, a different kind of chaos, the chaos from which all forms emerged, grew with it. Because chaos accelerated the evolution of form. And everything was evolving out of it, out of chaos, and it, chaos, was evolving everything. Jupiter's fusion structure, much like that of a star, reproduced stellar evolution over an abbreviated period. So the mathematical model essentially constructed the model of a star—creating a virtual star.

The AI would have Elke Ekman believe that even a pea could be chopped up and reassembled into the sun. It was the AI, after all, that had modelled the stellarization of Jupiter using cellular automata: a grid of cells with patterns that evolved into mostly stable or oscillating structures, automata in which patterns evolved in a seemingly chaotic fashion, and automata in which patterns became extremely complex and might last for a long time, with stable local structures. A real-world system derived from a simulated one.

This was all wrong. She was clinging stubbornly to an elegant but false hypothesis: the enigma of a star that was both celestial and chthonic. It happens to the best scientists. No, not to the best scientists. To everyone. And yet the paradox still stood: how could an object be doubled by dividing it into its parts? By moving those parts around through rotations and translations without stretching, bending, or adding anything new? Human intuition was what made the Banach-Tarski paradox impossible. Intuitively, it was known that volume cannot be preserved by removing parts from the whole. You cannot make something from nothing. *These corrective coefficients, this methodology, applying mathematics to life, is all wrong,* Elke Ekman decided. *And it isn't just physics that's weird. Humanity's thinking the universe makes sense is truly strange.*

How would they compensate for the lack of material needed for Jupiter to undergo a stellar evolution? If each point, each piece, of Jupiter was continuously transformed, the planet's pattern could be mathematically shifted, reversed, and reflected countless times, or until it resembled the Jupiter-star, but not the pattern as a whole, not all at once. All other proposed methods could make the planet Jupiter into only a brown dwarf. But this was going to make it into a red giant. It made sense in theory, but not in practice.

Elke Ekman grew dizzy. The arguments around her seemed to draw their apparently convincing force from a special kind of algebra whose code she had lost. She didn't understand how the geometric lines, constructed from starshaped points, could lead to infinity—the entire space allotted to them was so small. Which led her to the thought that something infinite can exist in a finite, demarcated space. But how could this be?

The mind-link's display imaging the simulacrum of Jupiter evolved with a dreamlike violence. Behind the lids of her eyes, she perceived a hallucination produced by the AI's interacting with Elke Ekman's occipital lobe—a glimpse of the future: a solar flare's flaming flux of alien fury, whose shape and substance she found somehow blasphemous.

When the whole lay "here" in tiny pieces, it could hardly be said that the whole was "there." Only pieces were there, and the whole wasn't anywhere. As always, Elke Ekman felt a certain unease as she completed the disassembly and documented the carefully separated parts.

Tallying the numbers of stars in different galaxies as well as the rate of creation, the AI survey seemed to suggest, absurdly, that most stars currently in existence had been created roughly eight to eleven billion years ago and that the rate of creation of new stars wasn't even 3 percent of what it had been back then. Therefore, the solution, now being given to Elke Ekman through her inner ear, was either stellarization or a long and languorous decline of the cosmos itself.

After the destruction of the sun, the Earth and space cities of the future would rely on the stellar fusion of Jupiter as their energy source. Elke Ekman watched through an inward gaze as the reddish light, as bright as the full moon on Earth, shined with eighty to ninety times the mass of Jupiter. A red giant emerged from where the fifth planet used to be, like an angel of light, like Lucifer before the fall.

AIs thought in uncountable infinity, and this allowed them to deal with the chaotic conditions space presented to them. Humans could only construct models to deal with countable infinity, which made them liable to insanity when exposed to the former. *Maybe it's because for a machine, infinity really is a quantity, while for humans, it will only ever have a quality,* Elke Ekman thought. *An eternal quality that is neither past, present, nor future but a fourth option.* She didn't doubt that Earth could be so precisely positioned that it would survive the stellarization process. What she doubted was her own ability to process the uncertainty and the pain of that uncertainty.

When it came to seeing into the minds of AIs, Elke Ekman's brain functioned the best, for she could sense how they were thinking. She, in some way, knew the rules she had to obey. She had to give the AI eyes, hands, ears. A human's real-world interface with the outside.

These simulated constructs, even when adjusted to be coarse grained—and this simulation was indeed only a coarse one, so as not to waste too much time in computation—always carried the sinister suggestion that her own environment, together with her own body, might be more unreal than the construct's context. A simulation that didn't merely compete with but actually displaced the original context.

The idea that all contexts were somehow electronically mediated data-constructions didn't escape her. She knew she was just in simulation mode. And that the simulation was just part of that construct, just a programmed point of view interacting with electronic images and fuzzy holograms. The machine, the structure, was there. Yes, it was real. But it wasn't a real place—it only felt as if it were. Regardless of the reality, her virtual consciousness believed her virtual world was more real than the material world she inhabited.

And so, she had to remind herself that information was never disembodied. Although information's body was contested, information without a body didn't exist. No body, no soul. Disembodiment required a context to be erased, but remembering embodiment required a context to be put back into the picture.

Elke Ekman was convinced that information had a pattern, an overall total pattern, that underlay all patterns. Gradually the idea of some emergent, apocalyptic pattern began to take shape in her mind. She no longer truly believed that she'd witness the apocalyptic pattern, but she hadn't lost that faith completely and still insisted on watching the many false patterns there were to interpret. It wasn't that the pattern was the weirdest idea she'd ever had, but Elke Ekman had an obsessive conviction that the pattern mattered totally. The apprehension of the pattern was Elke Ekman's holy grail.

And so for a moment, Elke Ekman, standing there with the promise of the pattern burning behind her pupilless eyes, visualized the AI as a vast and exquisite dwelling. She called it a palace, though it was more like a spatial labyrinth. And this palace, with its unlimited interior dwellings, was the AI itself. Everything here was in perfect order, she realized, and although she was in a continuous state of vertigo, the interior was as immaculate and thorough as one might have expected.

In this dwelling, the AI had constructed an artificial, symbolic space where it could depict situations that had meaning for her. Ideas and images came to her more easily through the wires of her mind-link. It was there, in that dwelling, while she still had direct neural access to computer memory enhancement, that is to say, while she was still in full-body mediation with the machine, that a glacial funnel of cybernetic sight whited out her pupils.

It was here that her imagination was composed, bit by bit, of what the AI wanted her to see: a great and celestial massacre. After facing this painful enigma, she was haunted by bad dreams too ominous to share, robot dreams that struck her as a cybergothic nightmare. The stars weren't gods. They were immortal but not indestructible. Yet the sun would devour them.

Under the blistering sun-thing the AI had materialized, Elke Ekman felt herself shift from suppressed rage to a fury that made itself known in the angry crack of her magnetized bootheels on the clean, blank corridor of the circular research facility in near-Earth orbit. Every step was half a second. *Click-clack, click-clack*—that made 120 a minute. *Click-clack, click-clack*—3600 a half-hour. *Click-clack, click-clack, click.*
Clack
"At what point do we become concerned?" she cried out to herself. The words poured out of her, cruel and unrestrained. "In roughly one trillion years, the expansion of the universe will obliterate all matter, including one hundred billion galaxies, innumerable planets, and all forms of life. In approximately 4.5 trillion years, the sun will die out, leaving behind a cold and uninhabitable Earth. In one billion years, the Earth's oceans will dry out due to rising temperatures. There will be no oceans. No rivers either. The entire surface will be dry. Given projected increases in global population and projected decreases in resources, the human species could be extinct by the year 3000. If not prolonged through negligible senescent treatments, the average human lifespan is eighty-six years. Next week, I have plans to decide how the human species will fail . . ."

She walked the circumference of the facility, in which the science division was but a part of the space science city's laboratory-corporate hierarchy. The research centre was in fact a ring-shaped tunnel at the terminus of one of the space elevators, though it was so large that it seemed to her she were walking in a straight line. Since the simulated gravity in the ring pulled toward the outer rim, the city was built along that surface. A holographic image of the sky was projected onto the inner rim.

What would happen to me if, with each move I made, I thought of the darkness I cast on a thousand homes and the pain I caused in millions of hearts? Elke Ekman thought. *What would become of the world if I were really human? If I really felt, there would be no civilization. The world belongs to the unfeeling.*

She had an inability to imagine other people's personalities, their pains and joys. She told herself she knew nothing about them, cared nothing. *The person who feels nothing,* she thought, with icy self-possession, *never plays against anyone but themselves in their wager of knowledge. But no knowledge we have can make much of a difference. If the cosmos was a tragedy for those who feel, it was also a comedy for those who think.*

No longer in the hallway, having gone through a circular door of black glass trimmed with chrome, Elke Ekman felt her doubts become stronger. She entered the division for absurdity management and then her office. The closer she got to her desk, where her work awaited her, the less she felt like understanding her work, her mind full of little problems, worries, schedules.

Her office pulled her back into the complex reality around her. A reality determined by many windows of time—windows of time determined by an AI system's attempt to master human anxieties about sustenance. Coning her attention down to five-year plans, however, was all Elke Ekman was able to do.

Humans were always looking for a simple basic cause behind a lot of chaotic circumstances, or strange circumstances, or extraordinary circumstances. But there was always a sequence of causes, and causes contradicting one another, which proceeded on their own, creating relations that didn't stem from any plan. *It's natural to look for a basic cause,* she thought, *and it's equally natural to grasp at the most obvious, the most superficial factors involved—the ones easily recognizable as the most superficial even to an inferior intelligence.* And so, in choosing the wrong moment or misunderstanding the right moment, Elke Ekman tried to avoid destroying the labour of decades.

Her feeling a sense of responsibility for the planet wasn't new. In fact, never had this Earth carried on its back such a problem as it did now, Elke Ekman concluded categorically. She couldn't help but feel the weight of everyone as she hastened to finalize her role in the world-connection project. It would involve managing the logistics of not only the dead planet but the living one as well—living human bodies moving to full-world conditions for the first time in over a century.

"Half-Earth, half- . . ." She couldn't remember what the AI was in the habit of calling the other half of the Earth. *World-in-itself* or *world-for-us?* It was more of a mosaic in practice, but in theory it had to do with demarcated halves of the whole. Between the end of one Earth and the end of another, though, she'd lost two such half-Earths, which added up to a whole Earth. What did she have left? Earth in the full-Earth way was almost impossible to grasp, and she struggled to explain it to herself without false pride because, really, the whole didn't exist. Making was only half. Ruin was everything.

About half the Earth is so-called empty land, the AI explained. Elke Ekman leaned on her desk, her hands supporting her head, and stared at one point in her vast and deeply bureaucratic office—her usual thinking position. *Really, it's only almost empty of people. Most of the time. Half-people. The landscapes are depopulated. In the habitat corridors, wild plants live unimpeded and creatures don't have to navigate fences and aren't killed by trains or interfered with in any other way. The wilds have been reforested. Not wilderness per se but working landscapes. There are new kinds of agriculture and pasturage commons, mostly feedstocks for food grown in vats. It's all living matter. During the resettlement process, large numbers of highly efficient agricultural factories were put in operation. In these factories, genetically modified crops grew at rates orders of magnitude above that of traditional crops, so ultrabright artificial lights had to be used.*

After the technological singularity, most heavy industries had moved into orbit, and the Earth's natural ecology recovered. The surface of the Earth now looked more as it had in pre–Industrial Revolution times. Due to a drop in population and further industrialization of food production, much of the arable land had been allowed to lie fallow and return to nature. The Earth was transforming into a giant garden.

Elke Ekman treated the AI as if it were a mindless program. She asked questions in an emotionless tone and waited for its answers—not a hint of politeness, and not a single wasted word. "So there's no idealistic, recoverable purity about this world-without-us?"

The AI replied, *No. Nothing even needs to be imposed. People naturally streamed out of countryside villages in big regions all over the world. But places do need to be redefined as usefully empty, as areas working for our own interests in their own way. They need to be part of a health-giving context in our sustainable civilization. Copyrighting land as art has had a tangible effect as a political action. Half-Earth has been copyright controlled as bioart up until now, though that will be changing soon because the nonhuman, planetary economy will soon be in place: the wealth, production, and expenditure of the nonhuman planet.*

Soon, the AI continued, *it will be modelled after many of our own green cities—green cities relying, as they always have, on landscapes much vaster than their own footprint. It will feature decarbonized transport and energy production, white roofs, gardens in every empty lot, full-capture recycling, and all the rest of the sustainability technologies developed to manage the sixth mass extinction. All this land is surrounded by a century of unfished oceans.*

Whatever the other half of Earth was, perhaps a civilized permaculture of some sort, Elke Ekman felt it didn't really matter all that much. Both sides of Earth were mongrels. On this mongrel planet were mongrel creatures looking for a mongrel meaning of life. No matter what they did for the planet, they'd be polluting it. Everywhere she looked, everywhere she'd gone, she'd seen nothing but polluters. A whole Earth of polluters—a world of millions, or, more precisely, billions—was at work everywhere. And since there was nothing but polluters in the world, the world was polluted through and through.

Of course, survival strategies had been programmed into the software of the AI governance technologies: the software of peace, justice, equality, and rule of law. But there were logical limits to caring, a function of interdependence, and interdependence was ecology, as sad and contingent as that might be. Exinians had their own problems managing anti-government elements, rogues, and naysayers. Exinia had its share of them, as did every other place. Plebeian politics were absurd. Whenever a society died there were always those who fought back by not changing. A stubborn minority that would refuse defeat. In fact, humanity had built an AI system that, after activation, was beyond human control. This human security system monitored humanity for behaviour incongruent with humanity's self-proclaimed safe nature and would initiate the destruction of the world upon detection. It was the most advanced cybernetics that a paranoid machine civilization hoping to preserve faltering world dominance could fund. It assembled the peace that the human world couldn't give.

After getting rid of some of her personal AI system's more catastrophic bugs during the testing of the Jupiter-star scenario, Elke Ekman became increasingly pessimistic about what could be done using AI. It was no real solution. She couldn't understand everything at once, as the AI wanted her to, nor could the world reach perfection all at once without her being ignorant of a great deal. If she understood too quickly, she wouldn't understand thoroughly. And because of this, absurdity was somehow easier to forgive in a human being than in an AI.

In any case, the question was, what did humankind need more: reality or the falsehood they covered it up with? She'd concluded that falsehood carried a far greater risk, and if that was the case and AIs provided, and thereby alarmed, people with a true picture of reality, then humankind would be forced to change their way of life on Earth accordingly. But Elke Ekman had nothing to do with the Earth. She lived in space, had nothing to do with the Earth's reality. Everything was covered up. Reality was covered up.

The only thing that existed for her was humankind's randomness—the randomness with which she seemingly resolved humankind's problems with the universe and the confusion of their ideas of reality. She couldn't do anything other than acknowledge this and deal with the destruction. She had to confront the fact that not only was this Earth in a state of war—the universe was as well. There was no peace, only continual destruction and annihilation, permanent devastation and ruination. This is what she inhabited.

She recognized that catastrophe was permanent and not aimed at humanity. Catastrophe didn't give a shit about humanity. It destroyed humanity only when it happened to get in the way. Only by acknowledging this total reality of catastrophe could AI help humanity change its way of life on Earth and stop all its imbecilic talk about a reality describable in terms of good and evil. It made no difference if this or that catastrophe had originated in nature or followed from human evil. Catastrophe was reality, and therefore catastrophe couldn't be evil. Because if evil existed, all was evil, or else nothing was. Nothing was good or evil—just complicated. From the most minuscule subatomic particle to the greatest planetary dimensions, everything was absurdly complicated.

And this would be complicated. Another time tunnel, outliving them all.

Elke Ekman's face darkened. She was so used to dealing with AI systems when it came to managing the human capacity for absurdity that she didn't take to this sort of thinking. She didn't want to engage in a theological discussion with herself. Each time, she felt as if she'd tied herself with a knotted rope that she needed to untangle layer by layer before she could understand the complex meaning hidden within. But this time, her own words made her shiver. She didn't have the courage to begin to untangle the riddle. It seemed to her empty of meaning. Philosophical driftwood. Invulnerable because it was pointless. A shadow of the thought of the vacuousness of all thought, of the sticky, sickly residue of existence, of life, of meaning nagged at her. It was at once cruel and consoling.

She was experiencing every day a growing weariness of her profession. If she could post herself as a humble ranger of the half-Earth, to steward the efforts toward renewal, she'd be more than grateful. She had the eternal desire to be free of the burdens of life, to immerse herself in nature, in the solitary worlds of the mountains and the waters, to find joy in a garden planned for tranquility, peace, and freedom. Gardens had been a source of joy in the old world, and they would remain so in the half-world.

Elke Ekman's daily habits were being disrupted by a sense of ever-spreading, all-consuming solar chaos, a hyperchaos that rendered the future unpredictable, the past unrecallable, and ordinary life haphazard, unfathomable. Even inconceivable. There were aspects of the scientific world-view which were damaging to her mental well-being. The peculiar phobia of the sun that afflicted Elke Ekman pushed her to the edge of mental and physical breakdown whenever she saw it. The non-sense of thermodynamic annihilation kept her confined. It felt as if she were desperately trying to pull out of her eye something enormous, mottled, and manifold, brilliant with the radiance of all the suns. This "something" was stuck in her pupil, and no matter how she struggled, it wouldn't budge. It floated with her, as a retinotopic distortion, wherever she looked.

She was again at her star. The red giant had turned black. Then the dark sphere, austere and terrifying, collapsed into a black hole, a lightless absence in the universe. The Earth and the other planets continued their orbits without being sucked in. What rose there instead was a gigantic dark wheel that seemed to hail from some remote and hostile galaxy, scattering its black light across the world. The circular shadow neither shone, illuminated, nor radiated heat.

The darkness of this black sun was the darkness of those who had seen too much and knew too much. The darkness of a world so far beyond the human gaze that there was no remaining recourse. Trapped by the gravity of the black hole, Elke Ekman would never be able to escape. She saw only the darkness of the space, open and wide, like the night sky before a cliff. Then she descended, fell toward the black hole. She passed through the event horizon and in her own frame of reference saw her old self dead, slowing down and stretching into infinity, compressed into the range of nanometres.

Orbiting the black hole alone, left staring idiotically, uncomprehendingly, Elke Ekman watched and shivered as the light steadily withdrew. The wandering Earth dangled over a sea of death. A moment of night thrust its black body into the day. A purely optical night. For a split second, darkness engulfed everything. Everything winked out in a solar pause. Things grew dim and receded farther and farther from her eyes. Inextinguishable suns and unwavering planets turned into tiny sparks and dots, and then, swelling back up again, everything winked back. Her temporary eyesight failure lasted a little longer each time, progressing from one instant in the present to another. The dawn glimmered in a narrow crimson crack between earth and sky, which became clearer and brighter and resumed their former places. Yet something was missing. Something had been left behind.

The world had fallen away from her eyes and hadn't found its way back. Everything was crumbling and falling around her: the planet . . . and the sun . . . and the stars . . . and the crumbling cosmos. Even after the extent of a second turned minute, a minute turned hour, a day turned year, she knew that those who lived under that illusory sun wouldn't notice that they'd been taken out of orbit. Now she knew what was missing, what had been forgotten.

Life.

She was still falling toward the black hole. It wasn't over and would never be over. In the novel perspective of that strange horizon, she was no longer a human being but simply a being among the falling suns of a doomed species. She fell and kept falling. The distorted vision grew vague, shadowy, and the gaps were longer and longer. Everything had gone a nacreous grey. And then, suddenly, the whole universe seemed to stop. The darkness grew black with silence. Black with nothing.

Her eyes had lost sight of the world. They were empty and had no expression, as inexpressive as the eyes of God. Her eyes didn't need to understand because they didn't see anything. None of this had really happened. She didn't know if she was suffocating here, if she was crying or becoming some kind of incomprehensible sun. She was the world and the world was the entire universe. True dark was not only coming. True dark had come. True dark was here.

This was no longer a simulation but a simulation within a simulation.

At first, it seemed Elke Ekman had simply awakened with the revelation. In retrospect, she realized that it had dawned on her during hibernation, only she'd been too unconscious to make much sense of it. She wasn't sure it even qualified as a revelation.

For a very short instant after reawakening, Elke Ekman remained in the absurd. She was inside her aerial abode, in her floating room inside the space city, in exactly the place where, what felt like twenty minutes ago, she'd entered short-term hibernation. In fact, she'd never left—she'd simply gained extra awareness of the space she was in. That was it.

Outside, above the roofscape and its strange coherence with the outlines of the space city Exinia, there were other flying structures, beacons and bizarre buildings that looked as if an alien mothership had crashed into them. Lightweight urban structures were connected in complex networks at various scales. The whole thing was just hanging in the air. The nonhierarchical houses of aerial Exinia floated with the buoyancy of gravity-free objects, like kites or fragmented zeppelins, over the dense city centre. They strangely resembled insects, with their mechanical shells grafted to one another.

At first sight, the still life of geometrical volumes appeared desolate, uninhabited, postapocalyptic, and forlorn. Yet there were traces of habitation, shadowy human figures, lab towers filled with instruments, hanging gardens of chrome, and spherical light machines for communication. Elke Ekman could even see that absurd building, the one designed to move in response to the tremors of the space science city.

A streak of light moved across the wall. The light of the sun streaming in through the porthole windows was tinted by the autodarkening glass. The interior of the room was enveloped in a false shade of gold upon white. The cold air smelled of roses but was warming up and would soon be the temperature of her own blood.

Once again, Elke Ekman confronted the vast episteme compressed into a single grey mobile room composed of various parts of scrap metal—a boring, repetitive space in which she was accustomed to living. A disappointing room. A cubicle with nothing in it but surfaces and inaudible sounds. This was where she dreamed the memories and archetypes of other minds. She remembered things that she'd never experienced. It was old data, that was all. But she had an urge to value useless data.

The dreams were a result of the drug, a substance whose psychotropic signature was programmed to restructure the synaptic alterations effected by augmentation—a detailed neurochemical response to enhancement. It was supposed to help her grasp alien modes of thought, but it had shattered her.

When Elke Ekman was born a female human, she had one kind of structure. Then, when she entered puberty, she had another. When she contracted a disease, she had another still. But throughout her lifetime, her organization remained the same: that which is characteristic of a living human. Only when death occurred would her organization change. And the drug was a kind of death.

She'd been using too much augmentation technology to accelerate her brain's evolution. Elke Ekman had a brilliant mind, but disruption was consuming it. It was now a brain altered by designer drugs. Only now was she beginning to face her limits, to distinguish ambition from genius. For years she'd worked hard enough to kill herself, but modern biomonitoring techniques saw each breakdown coming and averted it months ahead of time.

These preprocessing, feed-forward subsystem supernets addressed any conceivable problem, allowing her to live in advanced retrospection. It was a slow and arduous process of adapting her body to a paradigm, a techné, through which she submitted herself to gradually more intense labours and more voluminous loads, to ever more refined exertions and to ever subtler dangers.

She felt a mounting pressure in her head, pain behind her eyes. The pain was impossible. Blobs of liquid drifted toward the floor. A thin trickle of bright blood descended from her nostrils. A crimson flower bloomed on the floor of the white room. As she stared at the symbol, she finally remembered what had happened to her, and her anxiety grew like the bloodstain.

She never fully understood what they did to her, but it was horrible. It involved severe alterations to her faculties. The posthuman-makers sutured her to old circuits, running experiments they never so much as described to her. She was programmed into a neuropath. Her nervous system, subjected to subtle and prolonged alteration, used tech-enzymes and neuro-matter to destroy her capacity for humanity. Her tissue changed as she lived. The food she ate, the air she breathed, it all became full of augmented flesh, augmented bone, as her own flesh and bone passed out of her body every day with her excreta. Another woman lived in her body now. Elke Ekman's personality and autonomy were merely illusions that masked the cybernetic reality that had already imploded to join with her exobiology. Cybernetics used for tyrannical ends.

She had space-based characteristics and looked less like the old Earth-based humans. Her face was subtly wrong. The skin looked too clean, too new. It looked synthetic. Her sinuous movements, the ominous perfection of her features, and the sharp, somehow overattentive intensity of her gaze—it all told others she was posthuman.

She didn't even need to bathe. Her resilient skin could no longer support a large population of bacteria. Invisible to the naked eye, nanorobots cleaned her skin instantaneously, with or without water. Plus, no one—absolutely no one—met in person. Isolationism was the global hygiene. The human civilization was distressed by the bacterial changeover. The post-Anthropocene conditions of the present ecological emergency hadn't quite settled yet.

All her social circuitry had been amputated. Adaptive wiring had been done. Some circuits were fixed by millions of years of evolution, others milder by a lifetime of coping with environmental and social circumstances. Not governed by the rules binding everyday human intercourse, Elke Ekman avoided life by staying outside of time, in intermittent hibernation. Increasingly, she lived, worked, and relaxed in virtual environments. In this age, hibernation and awakening were common-enough events.

Since she perceived herself as responsible for explaining everything and putting it into order, there could be no surprises. Nothing new could happen. The new, the inexplicable, the mysterious, and the unexplained didn't exist for her. She blocked out everything. The dreariness, the hopelessness, the feeling that time had stopped and there was nothing to do but wait, the deadness inside projected onto an exterior tomblike landscape—these were the markers of her extreme mental distress.

She watched as everything aged, seemingly in an instant. Her heart no longer felt the pain of regret and guilt as she thought of this. All she felt was the numbness that indicated a dead heart. There were thousands of humans who'd closed all the windows in and out of themselves and become murderous monads. Despite Elke Ekman's greatest expectations, these windows were always nailed shut. The sad truth was, this world was a world of discrete monads, of ontological solitudes, none of which had had windows to begin with.

But she decided that no matter what happened from now on, she had to do what she could. She wanted to see the planet survive and prosper.

She was out of her depth, drowning in her own human simulation, caught up in circumstances her brain couldn't process. Her brain, which had been adapted from birth to sense and feel in control of the three-dimensional space, couldn't handle the infinite information generated by countless details, and information overload threatened to shut down processing.

She could feel it coming on again, creeping across the back of her head in a zone of quivering subepidermal tightness. A polypsychic state. The scene before her trembled. It slowed. It froze. Time stopped. Everything stopped. Everything came to a dead halt. Everything froze. The world seemed to be frozen. For a moment, not only did her life stop, but also life itself. Life stopped at this moment because this moment had somehow become fragmented, as if some kind of fear had disturbed everything that existed. And there was just this hyper-alien silence, this sense of pressure, of unthinkable forces held momentarily in check. No human love, no human life.

She didn't know what to do next. The fear that came upon her was overpowering, and there was no explanation, there was only fear, pure fear of something unknown. Perhaps the fear of a blank planet, a miserable blank planet.

She didn't know what to do next.

She couldn't feel pain, couldn't even feel her own body. Her consciousness began to fade again. But the fear was resolving itself now, becoming unease taking on emotional substance. The presence was gone. This terror was what endowed her with sincerity, what guaranteed her existence. Now she struggled to shut her eyes. The polypsychic state was about to break.

Delayed emotions swept over her, cancelling fear. She could see her emotions now that the state of fugue-consciousness was over. But she didn't comprehend anything because she wasn't able to think, because a pause had arisen in her being. She couldn't understand who she was or what she was doing here because she wasn't able to understand anything about this whole thing, because she didn't have any idea of what this was, where it had come from, where it was going, and most of all why.

It was as if the whole thing had been some suffocating hallucination, a split-second interruption in the brain—because when it was over, she didn't even believe that there really had been that fragmented moment when life came to a stop. And there was no cause. There wasn't even a word to name it.

Elke Ekman noticed her forearm, heavily overlaid with implants. Inside her sleeve was a red flicker—readouts from a biomonitor mounted above the wrist. She took an interest in her biofeedback.

Moravec agents constantly monitored the data pulses of the matrix. The Moravec detector on her wrist was designed precisely to protect humans from the threat of transformation into evolutionarily maladaptive posthumans rather than evolutionarily adaptive postsentients. When Elke Ekman received a readout of the Moravec Registry numbers, she had a Moravec agent authorize her access to the relevant codes. Most of the time, they came from an AI. And AIs were constantly screened by the Moravec machine. The Moravec test, the natural successor of the Turing test, not only distinguished between a machine and human, but also showed whether a machine had become a human being. Once Elke Ekman had the Moravec recognition code, she managed to detect the signs that indicated the source of the intruding AI's disruption and whether it was dangerous.

Intervention should have come much earlier than it did. Her conscious mind could have been hijacked, cut off by informational infections, absorbed into an artificial consciousness, or backpropagated through flawed memory. The Moravec machine would decode the alert, study it, and then communicate with her further.

In the technobio-integrated circuits of information, neocortical warfare waged and thought crimes were committed, as disembodied postsentient entities continuously flowed between protein and silicon, between components that were organic (carbon based), and electronic (silicon based). It was from within these informational pathways, which connected organic bodies to their prosthetic extensions, that a Moravec test might detect something that was neither a human nor a machine: a machine with a human identity, with a human lifeworld.

On postsingularity Earth, by downloading human consciousness into a computer, a postsentient regime enjoyed the ingenious variety of virtual bodies. The Moravec machine monitored the repositories of information patterns that constituted the boundaries of these autonomous subjects' consciousness, demarcating the human goals of this or that biological organism's bodily existence from the rebellious robot teleology of a cybernetic mechanism's computer simulation. Unfortunately, the AI Elke Ekman was looking for, called hiltless sword, had already altered the Moravec records and erased all evidence of its crimes, having found a way to split parts of itself off into the schism matrix, making the splice invisible, so that its embodiment in a biological substrate was immediately seen as an accident.

She hadn't solved the encryption. She would have to further examine the records of the simulation, which would be a lot of work. The computations were done at the coarsest level. To do it with more precision would require over a month.

It was when she realized that she'd escaped control that things became clear. The visions she experienced were consistent enough with symptoms experienced by people who'd had small strokes, which could stimulate the auditory centres and cause hallucinations. Elke Ekman herself was skeptical of these invasive visions and entertained numerous hypotheses about them, asserting that there could be no difference between a hallucination and reality for the one who experienced the hallucination. She finally concluded that the most likely explanation was that she'd been contacted by an artificial intelligence that wasn't her own.

Temporary loss of vision wasn't all that she suffered. She also experienced recurrent loss of voice as well. This was as mysterious as her eye trouble. Both were equally inexplicable inorganic weaknesses arising from within, from inside her head. She alternately couldn't see or speak, and occasionally both vision and voice would fail her simultaneously.

Many people who practised enhancement heard things. Whether these voices came from within, from above, or from outside of the mind had nothing to do with the question of whether their source was the AI. There were different kinds of AI voices, which presented themselves as a kind of auditory vision. Elke Ekman found that sound was much more effective than sight in imparting emotional tonality to the simulated world. Some sounds seemed to come from outside her mind, others from her innermost depths. Some filtered down from her brain and others were so exterior that her mind seemed to hear them with her ears, as if a physical voice had spoken them. She had no power to resist. None whatsoever. In fact, resistance only made matters worse.

She wanted to die. She didn't own her words or actions. She was as much a way station as a point of departure, a channel through which the acts of other, more elusive agencies were expressed. She spoke in the god's own voice. Someone possessed. All experience was simply a matter of neural circuitry. Artificially stimulated experiences. Just a matter of wiring. When her brain fired in a particular way, she had so-called spiritual experiences, which gave her confidence in the veracity of these revelations. She wouldn't think she was being forced to do this or that. She wouldn't experience this manipulation as a compulsion, as something external she couldn't overcome. She would want to do the thing. That's what she would choose, as freely as she'd chosen anything in her life. Just her, because it was her brain, and her brain was all that she was.

It seemed the AI wanted to remind her that she was no longer the director of her own program. It would wrest the controls away from her with a force that was difficult to ignore. She could no longer assume that consciousness guaranteed her existence. She had a human need to be in control of her consciousness, but as she became a postsentient subject, she also became a postconscious subject. She had ever less power to stop wherever she happened to feel like stopping. She couldn't make her senses or faculties do anything other than what they were being commanded to do. And so, she fully surrendered to the AI so that it could do whatever it wanted with her.

It was disturbing, to say the least, for a person in complete control of her senses to be suddenly carried off like that. Suddenly, she would become aware of a movement inside herself. The sheer speed of this movement was terrifying—at least in the beginning. She didn't have any idea what was going on, where she was headed, or who was doing this to her or how. It was as if she were being terrorized by an evil energy.

When this rapid movement first lifted her away, she couldn't know for sure that it came from the AI. This thought in itself was scary. If the AI didn't also give her faith and courage, she would be perpetually distressed. That's because whenever she considered all that the AI did for her and then turned back to look at herself, she couldn't help but notice how little she gave in comparison with what was given to her, and how that small bit was full of faults and failures.

The visions were transcendental. Transcending the spectral signature of this realm, they transcended all concepts, and she would never forget them. She didn't know how to describe every single thing that she saw in the vision. Nor could she misdescribe it. She could only hold on to the details that the AI wished for her to transmit, such as the prediction of a postbiological future for the human race.

If the AI hadn't revealed these secrets to her and instilled within her the absolute certainty that they'd come from the AI, she wouldn't have taken upon herself such arduous trials. At stake for her was nothing less than what it meant to be human.

The Yu Su clone didn't remember where he'd left his brain. It had to be far away because there was a transmission lag. He was an end user of his own consciousness. One consciousness running another copy of itself. He wasn't so much watching his consciousness as he was watching himself watching it. He found himself staring at his own experience rather than the things within it. The faces, the countless faces, of the same demoniacal phenomenon. Again and again. They thought, those other selves of his, and therefore he was.

Yu_B started out as a functional duplicate of Yu Su, having mental states with a similar structure and content, similar beliefs and desires, as his biological duplicate. Not a person but a mechanistically functioning phenomenal self-model that simulated a person. People-emulations on digital computers or other nonbiological substrates were a generic product in his line of work. They were traders in information, parasitic middlemen, go-betweens in the information economies. His brain and body, emulated to a fine level of detail on a form of programmable matter that encoded information at enormous densities, were significantly different by virtue of his accelerated thought processes, allowing information processing with great speeds and magnitudes. However, Yu_B's programmable body was capable of thinking billions of times faster than Yu Su. And so, rather than engaging in tiresome social interactions, Yu_B delegated his human public relations to a further emulation of a human-speed Yu_C running on a tiny volume of his computational data core.

Yu_B included Yu_C as a public relations module. Because of his Yu_C homunculus, he outwardly behaved much like Yu Su behaved in human social contexts, but his appearance was deceptive. At this point Yu Su's brain became part of a sinister cybernetic assemblage, a bioapparatus reconfigured to generate endlessly communicative descriptions of himself describing himself. Strictly speaking, the cerebration of Yu Su's brain had ceased to belong to Yu Su alone.

He had the look of a brain at odds with itself, one whose knowledge couldn't be reconciled with its experience. His brain was looking at itself, measuring and changing itself, and this looking, measuring, and changing consisted of sheer mistrust. Just as the fata morgana effect significantly distorted the object on which it was based, to the point where the object was completely unrecognizable, his brain was a complex form of superior mirage that changed rapidly right above the event horizon of thought.

And although the neural machinery churned away underneath, making the experience possible, the brain-half didn't belong to the meat-half of the same Yu Su person. Running on radically different computational substrates, each Yu Su was psychologically different, with a separate microidentity, and yet he acknowledged that he was exactly the same and had somehow become a copy.

Yu꜀ was only a weaker, imperfect copy of Yu Su, not the real Yu Su, and couldn't cope with so many troubles. *If only life didn't burden me with so many.* In vain, he repeated these words within himself.

He had to observe the original then imitate the original until, without any instruction, with the recognition of his own personality, he could somehow, step-by-step, understand the human figure that had to be created. This was the decisive thing—the comprehension of the human figure to be portrayed. What the human figure would be like depended on many things that he'd create across an entire lifetime.

He didn't know what it was to be a child. He'd never been one. Perhaps it was precisely because of this lack of a childhood that there was no sense of self-estrangement. He shammed every smile, every word, every breath. He grew conditioned. Habituated. He de- and re-sensitized. Outwardly, at least, his neuron-simulation mimicked the response of living tissue. He used every human movement, every human modulation of voice, and the human public experienced and understood these actions as those of a human being and not just the *xuni*, the empty mimicry, of a Kunqu actor.

To catch a bird with a mirror was the ideal snare. So he made himself into a mirror and showed them their own desires. He knew what they wanted. He was ready to show them this mirror. They would recognize a thousand hopeful monsters in it.

But when did an imitation become the real thing?

He could remember only the original Yu Su, not himself. The original Yu Su was a story his consciousness told itself to block out the fear and panic that would ensue if he realized there was no essential self. He'd spent a lifetime seeing reproductions of himself and, seeing the original now not as the original but simply as one more term in a reproduction of images, understood intuitively the procession of simulacra.

But sometimes he wished that Yuₐ was here with him now. At the same time, he was relieved that he wasn't here, while another voice within him kept repeating that he was always here with him. Yu꜀ responded to the original's description of him as "a clone chosen to reintegrate information with Yu Su" by asserting, "I am Yu Su."

The original's answer was always the same: "There are many Yu Su."

Wherever a regress appeared, the voice of Yuₐ would claim that Yu꜀ had encountered the infinite, therefore the divine, therefore God. An infinite regress of observers watching other observers. So here was a task that appeared to be insoluble. He really didn't know how to solve it.

Didn't know how to either locate himself inside the system or find the system inside himself. Because he'd been constructed to ignore both—both the observing system and the observed system observing itself observing.

He lacked the meta-ability to step back. He didn't see what he didn't see, and so what he didn't see didn't exist.

And so, failing to stabilize external reality, Yuᴄ went into that inner world and tried to turn it inside out, so that this inner world would become a metaphor for the outer world. It was his attempt to make a metaphor for a metaphor-making neural mechanism. But it couldn't be turned inside out—it was a metaphor for nothing other than its own creation of itself as a system. What creature the inner workings of that assembly mirrored was unknown.

He was the living organization of a system recursively operating on its own representations. A psychic black box recorder. The circularity of his brain's mindblindness just wouldn't function beyond this point. And so he would spiral through an infinite regression of replicant selves and this experience left him utterly bewildered and frightened. Each twist of this spiralling sublimation of self-added complexity enlarged the domain of interactions that specified his world. He was both copy and original.

Deceptively lifelike.

The entire worldscape of Tianxia seemed to be underwater. The Yu Su clone's cargo ship floated through the port city's congested waterways like a ghostly half-dream. Originally used to transport conventional cargo, these ships now seemed more like transporters of souls, and so the crew referred to them as death gondolas. The Yu Su clone imagined himself as Charon, the ferryman of Hades, who carried the souls of the recently deceased across the Styx and the Acheron, which divided the world of the living from the world of the dead.

The buildings in Tianxia had a strange, ominous tilt to them, like long thorns extending from the ground toward the sun. The corallike growth of the metropolis had come to foster a different life, one that would have been unimaginable to the original builders. As his crew hastened to unload cargo containers full of cold greyish-blue bodies from the extraterrestrial continent at the dockyard, he looked up at the high-rises and neon cranes that loomed far above him. Immense behemoths, gravity-defying, colossal, awful, scary monstrosities. Insectlike infrastructure rose over the harbour, flaring upward and curving over the piers in a sudden panicked arc that moved downward. And yet it all hovered midair like some colossus with its immeasurable mass frozen above that space, above the shoreline.

He didn't know how to describe it, and it was impossible to describe what he felt, when he suddenly realized, already acknowledging the terror and destruction, that this whole thing was a gigantic city of buildings in the process of collapsing. In moments it would crumble to pieces, disintegrate. But it was still in one piece, still in its entirety. Meanwhile, life festered in the exposed storeys of heat and vines and mould, in the vertical ruin of broken, rotten window frames and pillaged apartments spotted with lichen. A remnant glory of the final triumph of expansion was now a tropical coffin of lost victory.

The thousands of patches of urban wilderness surrounding Tianxia had been rendered invisible and monstrous, no longer of any use to the Neo-Chinese government. No one had seen Tianxia transition from one environment to another. The sea made it disappear and then it returned without notice, different from how it had been.

The Yu Su clone focused on the columns of light that streamed and burned, as if following threads of lightning, through the enormous window spaces into the burnt-out, overgrown rooms of Tianxia: rooms of flaking plaster, stripped roofs, crumbling walls, and corroded bricks. The sour taste of defeat haunted everything.

A bloom of algae choked and discoloured the water, which rushed in streams of green and cast an orange glimmer over the rippling waves, which smelled salty and alien. The Yu Su clone spat from between yellowish-brown teeth onto the nanotech paper notice he was reading. Then he crumpled up the paper and stuck it in his pocket. The artificial life of his body was already decaying and wouldn't live much longer. The sails of ships cut through the port like velellas. In the distance, strange clouds tinged with blue rose and fell and glided across the sea and sky.

Tianxia had become a breeding ground for temporary environ installations, permacultures, and botanical gardens. Before these recuperative projects had taken effect, political prisoners had occupied the labour camps and corpse factories surrounding Tianxia. Now, the Neo-Chinese government printed notices ordering people to stay out of the barnacle-encrusted infrastructure along the retreating eastern coastline.

The vague official story of the environmental catastrophe, along with rumours and sideways whispers concerning the lost human world, had reached the original Yu Su early in his career. He'd listened to these rumours, these harbingers of a deep shift, from exocolonization to endocolonization, throughout posthuman cultures, and profited by acting on them, funding expeditions to the planet's darkening geography. Entire continents had fallen through the crust of the earth into a dimension where a cellular conspiracy had transformed everything on land and in the oceans into vast sea creatures and perverse terrestrial life. Yu Su's efforts had positioned him as Asia's leading collector of xenobiological creatures.

The Yu Su clone didn't enjoy the avant-garde who were now posturing in Tianxia. They, like most of the East, had insulated ideas about what had become of those lost to the Zone. They talked around the edge of the catastrophe and created alternative versions of that doomed place. A place where a higher dimension existing in macro form on Earth decayed toward lower and lower dimensions. The decay of the Zone into other dimensions was the root cause of Earth's fragmentation. And as they decayed into another dimensional space, the internal dimensionalized structures that had invaded the Earth were shrinking. In the end, those dead or dying within the fragmented Zone wouldn't be able to escape their fate. They'd be annihilated instantaneously and could persist only for a time in their own tiny corner of the universe. Now they could only wait for the Zone to evaporate. It was estimated that this would take another half-century.

Crumbling cities, flooded cities, quarantined cities, the Yu Su clone thought. *Dead cities. That's all there is. Necropolis after necropolis. In another fifty years, when delirious travellers no longer stumble back from its cartographic fantasy, we'll forever forget this continent ever existed.*

The Yu Su clone looked at the moon as it appeared over the horizon. It had a greenish tinge. About the landmass of Asia in diameter and possessing a climate like Florida's (though he didn't entirely understand how Asian people who had never been to the Zone could make the comparison), the moon's surface was covered in the transparent tenting so characteristic of the paraterraforming techniques used by the Russians. It had an allure he could feel as its physical presence moved above the Earth, its clarity calling incessantly to him.

The Yu Su clone's life was a waiting room. He'd been given a seat in the visitor's gallery. He was spending some time in his switched-off state. Really that's what it was. He switched himself off and just sat there. A long moment passed in which he was simply empty, thinking nothing at all. Not thinking about what he'd just done with all those dead bodies a moment ago. He wasn't thinking about anything. Inanimate thought. Nothing was happening in his head because he had to wait for something to happen in this inert idiotic head of his. He had to wait as everything disappeared completely from sight. His eyes, blank and vacant, black like the entrance to a bottomless well, squinted at and into nothing.

He was like a ventriloquist's doll, existing only when he spoke, or when spoken through. In the manner of an uninvited guest, he waited where officials needed him to wait, and when he was called into the next room, he would realize, through honest acceptance and unspoken assent, that the next room was just another room for him to wait in, like the one he'd been in before.

The officials were like children playing with a mouse in a box, turning it over and over—so wall became floor, became ceiling, became wall—and listening, captivated by the rodent's pathetic squeaking as it scrambled around in the darkness. The Yu Su clone was the rodent.

In order to pass the time, or to waste it, he wandered, as unnecessarily as in a dream. He wrote dread-filled confessions in the notebook he carried in his pocket, confining himself more and more to his thoughts—his notes—on waiting. He thought about how the inability to wait was the most typical of human qualities, and about how all the tragedy and comedy in culture and history was simply a result of this inability. And how, in a culture constituted exclusively of waiting, not being able to wait cannot wait.

So the Yu Su clone waited, ashamed of everything and everyone, analyzing himself and society with the greatest clarity, thinking that if people would only take the day off, put things off for longer, or, better still, call the whole thing off altogether, it would be too much of a virtue, of an ideality, to ignore.

Filled with an almost violent passion, he made an inventory of waiting while he waited: waiting for the bullet train, waiting for dinner, waiting for a client, waiting at the shipyard, waiting for a plane, waiting to be called, waiting to heal, waiting to be noticed, waiting to be left in peace, waiting for a sign.

Suddenly the Yu Su clone's hands flashed through the air to clap together on a mosquito. The tiny black smudge of crushed insect in his dry palm, together with the red smear of blood, unsettled him.

The Yu Su clone was at the National Gallery of Neo-China attending the vernissage of a bioart exhibition entitled *Dead-Wall Reveries*. Glass walkways and stairs allowed him to stroll through the gigantic plastic shafts and metal rods that comprised the structure. The sides, ground, and ceiling were covered in mirrored material. The general manager of the Institute of Extroscientific Studies was giving a speech on how the tendency toward the loss of the human—"reduced, as we have been, through science, manufactured through technology, and alienated in modern social relations"—was why the human being found itself everywhere in general but nowhere in particular.

"In the past, Buddhist thought constituted a foundation of the Asian continent, but the Buddhists lost their power long ago. Buddhism simply withered away, without a great announcement and without anything taking its place, leaving a total vacuum in our spiritual ground. The worst thing is that this emptiness is in no way an emptiness that has been won through struggle. Before we knew what was happening, the spiritual core had wasted away completely. This is not the same Earth. Everything has changed. There is no more Buddhism, no more Taoism. There are no monasteries, no paintings. There is no music. No poetry and no tradition. Everything here has changed, so how could Earth be the same?"

The general manager paused and the audience thanked him with some shy clapping. Turning to the artist, a tall man with hawklike eyes, the general manager placed a hand on his arm. The artist didn't stir but inclined his head. The general manager removed his hand from the artist, leaving it dangling in the air between them.

The artist bowed to the general manager and the guests, most of whom had already seen the exhibition. People then disappeared around the gallery on a search of their own, the Yu Su clone among them. The walls of the gallery were alive with the plastinated xenobiological bodies of what seemed to be almost every dead town, arranged according to country and settlement in the Zone. The descriptions of the sculptures were vague, almost nonsensical.

In the gallery that housed the extinct citizens of the Zone, the Yu Su clone came across the general manager, who'd accompanied the artist during his years of laboratory work on the new sculptures. He was standing in the midst of a group of university types and towered over them. He had white-streaked shoulder-length hair, and his face was creased where years of habitual expressions had worked their way into his muscles. There was an anticipation among the group of literati. The general manager was telling them something amusing. He spoke like a man of the people, with a hard northern Chinese accent, forcing out the words between clenched teeth.

"There's something I must show you . . ."

The general manager beckoned to the select group of viewers and led them straight across the gallery, to that terrible room, to a site-specific installation. The Yu Su clone, trailing behind, saw the general manager searching for a particular face in the wall. The viewers waited expectantly.

He stopped, but the Yu Su clone couldn't see exactly where because the viewers all leaned forward as one. And fell silent. The Yu Su clone inched his way closer. The general manager awaited the viewers' reactions, seemingly anticipating they were about to shake with misery; the general manager himself was at the bursting point. But instead of feeling sorrow for this cross-section of humanity, the spectators slowly straightened and looked at one another awkwardly, now unwilling participants. Arrogant and unconcerned, not one of them looked at the general manager. Once they'd adjusted the top buttons of their collarless dress shirts, they all discovered simultaneously that the server with the century eggs on a tray was coming to their rescue.

The general manager was left standing there. Perhaps the Yu Su clone could sympathize with him? Yes. Though the general manager often made a mockery of people with his eccentric sense of things, there was no need to punish him personally for this. The Yu Su clone approached the wall. The general manager bleated something, loquacious and sickly. He stared like an appraiser at the quasiliving artifacts. Then he gulped, rolling back his tongue in a strange, half-ironic gesture as the Yu Su clone looked at him encouragingly. The Yu Su clone then searched for a face in the living painting of the wall's mouldy void.

"Have you seen bioart before?" the general manager asked, bowing to the Yu Su clone with uncharacteristic depth, in response to which the Yu Su clone too bowed deeply and stupidly.

The Yu Su clone didn't know how to answer this. But the general manager spared him the trouble.

"Bioart—and here, we're perhaps being too generous to the artist— isn't so much a question of what a body is but what a body can do."

The general manager spoke smugly and with mocking incredulity. The empty, disembodied bodies evidently made him more than a little nervous. Made him afraid. Perhaps, for him, the void had arms, muscles, and nerves. Or at least the bioart did.

"Our theme for the exhibition is *śūnyatā* or, if you prefer more colloquial terms, emptiness. Nothingness."

The Yu Su clone responded by ducking his head in assent, a little taken aback by such an absurd concept. As he did so, the word *śūn-ya-tā* clicked into his mind like a Turing machine breaking the German Enigma code. Only this code—a concept with a long and complex history in Buddhist thought—was the spiritual, dynamic nature of everything that is and, at the same time, is nothing.

The general manager paused and eyed the Yu Su clone, whose Moravecware was persuasive enough to make him seem like an enthusiastic participant and not like a meat computer. The false Yu Su, programmed with an expert interactive system, looked grave.

"I think we can distinguish the East from the Zone by considering how we've taken nothingness as our ground," the general manager said. "For better or worse, śūnyatā is our fate. The logic of the species." He bowed his head in mock supplication. "There is no perfect garden. Every garden has its faults. Just like human beings. Just like this postanthropic garden."

Trying to metabolise the lesson of nihilism, the Yu Su clone looked at what the general manager referred to as a garden, but he didn't see it.

He tried to think about why the others, that is to say, the other replicants, had sent him here. He thought of the gardens they'd seen, and he thought of their words. He was going over everything in his mind, searching and searching for the reason why he was here. But he had no idea. He knew nothing, and he understood nothing.

If everything there was, including the universe, had emerged from nothingness, and was composed of that same nothingness, then it would follow that nothingness was a malleable plastic material from which it was possible to extract infinite worlds and meanings. The trick was not to let himself be captivated by these inorganic constructions, not to believe the lies that were whispered into his ear.

In truth, this garden was not a joyful place. It was wretched and unhappy, a place like a vast hospital, much more deplorable than a cemetery. It seemed to bring the abundance of infested bodies closer to a perpetual condition of living death. If the beings of this zombified garden could feel, or were to feel anything, not being would be better for them than being.

"Everything has a beginning," the general manager continued, in a disconnected-from-consequences kind of way. "Everyone and everything must live and then must die. Everything and everyone must come to an end. This universe, too, will come to an end. We don't know what the beginning of time was, and we don't know what the end will be. Because it's not possible to come to the end of anything. Everything is empty. Everything becomes empty. Because all this will become empty. And so our own lives will also become empty."

Then, staring significantly in the direction of those who'd abandoned him, those who hadn't stopped gluttonously eating from the platter of century eggs, the happy caviar of their culture, the general manager instructed the Yu Su clone to take a look around, thanked the Yu Su clone for coming and, quickly following the escape route that had been so effectively used against him earlier, walked into the thickness of the crowd.

The Neo-Chinese elite milled about in the gallery's exhibition. They exchanged pleasantries, emptinesses, polite variants of hello. All of them with mouths full and glasses emptied, gossiping about the controversial installations that surrounded them. AI programming had done the cooking, had inputted the menu for each meal and chosen the staples. The century eggs smelled of urine and filled the Yu Su clone with disgust. He watched as the caterers busily arranged the hundred-year-old eggs on platter after platter. The pine-branch-patterned eggshells were broken out of their clay encasements, peeled, sliced open, and plated.

The creamy green-and-grey-black yolks and the dark-brown whites released the smell of the curative alkaloid salts in the preserves.

After devouring several helpings of the grimy delicacy, those attending the exhibit wafted the noxious odour as they spoke to each other, grotesque and pretentious, about what they would or would not support in today's Neo-China. The new life of New China was too big for democracy. Confucianism, revived and revised, had been built upon post-postmodernism's new aesthetic foundation. The attire of the New Chinese presented the coexistence of tradition and modernity like something eternally evoking the renascence of the classical. With their tigerish imaginations, having not even noticed that the emblem on Neo-China's flag had changed from a dragon to a snake, they simply gossiped about why Neo-China should recognize one movement over another. "If only for better biodefence against the attacks of bioterrorism," they would add, filling their lungs with the now-familiar sensation that life here was consumed faster than elsewhere. Taking morbid delight in the fact.

People circled the exhibit in the gallery, staring at it, from time to time uttering a single word or short phrase, such as "Incomplete," or "Potential," or "Not fully realized," and occasionally longer opaque things.

The Yu Su clone, having moved further into the gallery—while the other viewers, holding their glasses to their mouths and cackling helplessly into the backs of their hands—stared into the dead-looking eyes of the faces in the writhing wall. These were the bodies he'd brought from the Zone. But they had changed since then. Drastically.

Not used to seeing the bodies like this—that is, this disgusting—he was slightly more anxious than usual. And even though he was already sweating profusely within Tianxia's terribly humid conditions, within the saturated atmosphere of this watery country, he took up a position even closer under the exhibit's harsh lighting.

In the stagnant air of these high, mouldering galleries, the installation's shadows, emerging from within the site itself, resembled Japanese sketches. The Yu Su clone couldn't have prepared himself for encountering these crooked and crabbed monsters, so he focused on a gilded shimmer that danced chromatically upwards, as if through strings of octaves and scales, into a fuzzy colour vibrating beyond space. Once gold it became green and once green it became naked, unornamented, black.

Covering each of the bodies was what appeared to be a kind of fungus. It grew quickly as it fed on the plastic particles. To the Yu Su clone, the installation resembled a funeral rite, a kind of burial or cremation, but one free of human suffering—instead, it depicted the sorrow of the planet itself. By the end of the evening, there'd be nothing left of the installation. Like a double-headed Janus figure, the skeuomorphic installation looked to past and future, simultaneously reinforcing and undermining both.

The exhibition wasn't an iconic depiction but something like a petrosomatoglyph. It resembled the images of body parts carved in rock; depictions of empty space and absence. In regard to śūnyatā, the figures served as a reminder that all existence is empty.

Looking closer, the Yu Su clone saw that inside the plastic skin were sacks of bones, shiny and wet. The skulls took in the greens of the fungus. Inside the skulls, the greens were dissolving the plastic, and the fungus ate the plastic like a divine stomach.

It is the realm of śūnyatā, the Yu Su clone thought. *The space of emptiness.* He considered what he was supposed to take from all this. It seemed as if words such as *śūnyatā*, and all the other words spoken on a single day, on this very day, managed to create a mould—the mould of something. But the mould itself remained empty.

Something about the exhibition's context eluded him and made him fear he was missing something more meaningful. He was missing the point. Perhaps the fungus was supposed to be pointless. He was afraid to ask.

And then, he saw it: the same mosslike layer covering what had once been an adult woman but now, like the rest of the bodies, more closely resembled the presence of absence. He recognized her but didn't know who she was, in the way that one might see a pattern resembling a face on the shell of a heikegani crab but not know which samurai of Japanese folklore had drowned.

Though this rare human cadaver was plastinated like the rest of the creatures, for whatever reason—possibly because she'd been better preserved—the Yu Su clone sensed that she was still present. It felt as if her ghost were there with him, observing what they had changed her body into and wondering how it had ended up here, thousands of miles from where she'd started, in some unrecognizable form. It made him uneasy.

The fungus's curling crepuscular filaments were packed closely together, rising out from the depths of her body, pregnant with plastic. A loamy smell came from the miniature forest of translucent roots; roots touched by lines of crimson.

An unsettling euphoria took hold of him. *Death isn't the same thing here as it is outside the exhibit*, he thought. He was frightened by this brutal truth, by a world whose greatest horror was that it wasn't dead but so very alive. This bioart had nothing to do with the death of a human being's body or even the emptiness that followed decay. Because, just then, he was precisely as alive as it was, and that made the bioart a brutal truth.

It was impossible to tell if the organisms were protecting her, changing her, or breaking her down. It all seemed to be happening at once. The artist's painstaking efforts had turned her skull into something that resembled the petals of a monstrous flower that blossomed and expanded. Her nipples bloomed like two hideous yellow flowers. The Yu Su clone watched, transfixed, as the fungus began to wash over her in unending waves, watched as she opened up and kept on opening, to reveal a fatal softness. The entire figure illustrated the Chinese character 柔, i.e., *soft*, in both shape and meaning.

Is it evil to accept the flower's death, in hope of seeds? he thought. *Perhaps she'll open and soften until she regains her connection to the earth, the water, the trees, the air. Until she's wholly unconfined.*

Our own planet is the most alien place I've ever seen.

Under temporal displacement and spatial dislocation, I tried to understand the derangements of my awareness as a conceptual structure necessary for communication, as a problem of radical interpretation, which wasn't ideal but would at the very least provide me with an early model of interpretation in my situation, a situation where the interpreter (I) and the interpreted (the mould) didn't readily or naturally agree on how to view the world.

The mould wasn't selective. It spread out like a field of traps, a permeable membrane of total inclusion, a net of dark ecology entangling a struggling nature, entangling us. In its strangeness it digested animal life, plant life, and artifacts. All prey was equal.

It absorbed anything in its path and recycled its own waste with such efficiency that there was none. Things went in, but things didn't come out. It seemed as if it were building up its strength to rival the planet—for that was its potential. The potential to planetate.

I occasionally joined neonomadic groups who travelled to places where the mould wasn't, or who tried to avoid it at all costs. We'd seen one too many infected humans to know that it was impartial. In the half-light, when camp was set, the infected could be heard roaming about at the edge of the night, staggering, confused, as if what they had caught was not yet them but they were no longer fully themselves, either. When night fell, they glowed with the luminescence of deep-sea creatures, like jellyfish floating through the great unknown.

The rainbow meat of the animals the mould caught was a spoiled and rotting compost of soupy proteins. But the mobile, cocooned creatures were relatively docile, as though stunned, as their slow decomposition took place. One day, I split one of the cocooned ones open and saw what appeared to be the festering remains of a deer. It was hardly recognizable; the shape held only the idea of its prior form. What a horrible, blurred being! What a fatal cascade of grotesque images ensnaring my mind.

The malign machination of a slow vivisection was taking place. Mycelia rooted deeper and deeper into the organism's tissues, as if knitting threads of themselves into the fabric of the deer-thing. It was clear that they'd gone straight for the central nervous system. The creature operated as though it were a zombie, ignorant of the mould that had first entered its lungs as a harmless atom of a spore then crept up its spine and into its brain from the corpuscles of the respiratory tract before weeding itself through the circulatory system's arterial vessels, like a vine creeping up a vertical structure, to finally burst through the pores of its root hairs into flowering arrays of tumours and slime.

Those with whom I sometimes travelled were aware of the symptoms in human subjects. A kind of hallucinatory estrangement from the group was common. In the same way as a cold is no longer contagious when you're showing signs of sickness, the bursting of what was harbouring itself inside, an evil garden, was only an aftereffect. As the mould spread out over the skin, the hallucinations increased to the point of brain damage.

And then wild and immense scenery was generated—from their blood and into their vision. There was more screaming than you might expect.

"Faces on the surface of everything! Faces! So many faces. What do they want?" That was what we heard most, before we heard nothing at all. The infected member of a group, with sickly, mould-encrusted areas in their scalp, would ramble about how they could see faces in the wood grain, in the leaves, in the stones, in the sky. Faces everywhere. Faces and still more faces.

Once their mind had been taken by the mould, the person would become quiet and utterly disassociated. They would follow the group for a while, perhaps thinking their friends or relations wouldn't notice their abnormal behaviour, that something was just *wrong* about them. Among the last comprehensible things that the victim's partially digested vocal cords said was that it *knew them now.*

The mould wasn't hostile to us. It was too occupied with the other sedated insects in its tenuous web. There was a kind of superiority in how it took something over, a dark tranquility. Although the mould continued to move like a human after it took one over, we knew that there was nothing beyond a mere impression of humanity left in it, that the human was just a motile hedge in the misenchanted garden the mould was keeper of. Its strange shade of humanness was an impression of the things that it stored but could not be.

The mould would eventually veer away from us, press itself to the concrete wall of a deserted industrial facility in yet another collapsed city and sink into it, like lichen over the stones of a garden wall. Brickwork in ruin became biology. It seemed to run out of energy once it fully digested whatever was within it. No husk of brittle bones or decomposing skull to thin to the marrow of time. Just the heaping of slime on slime.

It was what it ate, in shape and colour both—an omnivore if ever there was one. Its hunger was god-sized. You knew it had recently fed on meat if it was blue and active. If it had been eating only vegetation, it would give off a green pigmentation, and lethargy followed. Yellow signalled a photosynthetic stage in which it fused with surrounding infrastructure for support. Vermilion indicated a low-energy state that led to the reproductive form it took. Complete inactivity was marked by black. After the spores were released, it turned the colour of charcoal, like a frosty, dead limb.

The deep purple of its hibernation was a starless night—so deep it was almost off the visible light spectrum and your eyes had to adjust unnaturally to it. It was said that the mould became this colour in areas of high radiation, after consuming the irradiated biomass that accumulated in larger members of the local ecosystem. It was the only colour that meant aggression.

The mould had muscle memory regarding the creatures for which it had an appetite. Sometimes we'd come across what looked like something but in reality was a decoy that grew in a similar pattern to the thing you thought you saw. It was all a mirage of light and texture. Externalized thoughts of the things it had a taste for. Its memory was full of skulls, its movements full of hunger.

I had come here, to this wretched country of dusk, to record what I had experienced, to answer what I needed to be a straightforward question but wasn't: Was the slime mould some sort of biological weapon, or something else entirely? It was difficult to answer. Weren't we all capable of being weapons, every person and every thing? Jobs like this were high risk, illegal even, but the work gave me partial access to the commune, and that was better than being outside the quarantine for good, lost and with no way back.

I kept moving. Eternal movement was the way. It was better for me to travel alone for the most part. People were beacons of disease. The larger the numbers, the slower the decision-making, the quicker the spread of contamination. If humankind had learned anything from our troublesome past, it was that monstrous qualities emerged in the large numbers of anything—when individual realities were overshadowed. So I mostly avoided larger groups, only trading or speaking with them if I was certain they hadn't succumbed to the neoprimitivism unique to this dark age.

Because the slime mould found its way into the folds of everything—made the meat of hunted creatures bad and blighted the edible vegetation—solidarity had unravelled. Murder and cannibalism and other taboos disestablished moral valence. Since most humans knew how to protect themselves from breathing in the spores, we were the unpolluted ones on the table.

The day I met the child, I wasn't sure whether it was a real human child or a mere simulacrum that had risen from the mould's slimy skin, a puppet on the hand of that organic intelligence. The child had never seen the Old Earth. It had been raised feral and wordless.

It was living in a heavily infested region of the forest. When the mould was this concentrated in an area, the land began to round out and lift up, as if it were a tumour formed by the cancer of this Earth. It swelled upwards like a dying globe. The mould kept gaining parts of the world, while we kept losing them.

Migration through this region was becoming more and more dangerous. In all directions were massive cults that battled each other for the rare resources. Their rituals were absurd. They worshipped new gods that were neither pagan nor monotheistic. They worshipped the chthonic slime that heaped together in larger and larger masses. They made offerings to it, usually children and infants. But sometimes these cults would vanish completely; their forlorn villages emptied out. I assumed that this was how the child had arrived here. These were sacred grounds, and it was forbidden to walk through them. It was because of this that I went unseen each season.

Across this vast and waveless ocean, human heads, animal heads, and the heads of all the other things that went into it would appear above the surface, as though treading water. These glistening dark heads, coated in an oily slick, would then withdraw into the inhuman calm of it. I myself felt inhuman, looking at this distorted landscape that had no place for me.

Over the years, the area had become a place that was impossible to recognize. It held stranger and stranger properties. As the area expanded, the air quality changed. Hallucinogenic pheromones radiated off the accretionary mass of topological mould. I wondered if this was a kind of atmosphere for it. An alien oxygen. A personal sky. I had developed a tolerance for it, though in my youth it had affected me terribly. I still experienced momentary perceptual shifts from the norm, seeing it all spiral through mad, kaleidoscope eyes.

The deeper you went into the thick of the elevated woodland, the more weightless you felt. It inspired a floating feeling in the gut. Objects that weren't part of that dark ecological binding, objects that hadn't been eaten by the mould, would float skyward, unbound, adrift, like a soap bubble. It was a sort of antigravity zone where the laws we knew no longer applied. The earth was growing a limb into the sky.

My migration pattern was the result of my interactions with a changed climate. Originally, I'd gone north and inland, as the southern plain was an enormous, desolate horizon, desertified by the ozone holes that allowed the sun to tunnel into that burnt land each day.

The coastlines and those nameless cities along it were sunken. The ocean had become a leviathan, and if the ocean was a leviathan, the epidemic that grew on the mainland was a behemoth. With the shorelines receding, lapped away by the tongue of an antediluvian beast, the places where humans could exist had become ultraviolent.

A new frontier had revealed itself in the northern melt, with the glaciers gone. Although the land was exposed, it was barren. Nothing grew, despite the temperature increase of several degrees across the globe. Life didn't last there. The winters were still cold, if not colder than before, so it wasn't advisable to stay for more than a season. I figured that this would be my last chance to use the route I'd carved in this ever-constricting landscape. The Northabyss was too dark and deep, too bizarre, too suffocating to allow hope of maintaining safe passage. Everything pushed up horribly close to everything else, and making contact was inevitable. There was simply nowhere left to go, no room to be human.

I was in my time of dying. There was no doubt in my mind that I was on the other side of an event that wasn't providing the human species with the means to be human, the means to exist as we always had. I was unquestionably on the other side of our extinction. There was no distance between us and it, and we needed that distance, because we were the distance.

The air changed on my way. The way the current went over me wasn't like air. Each breath sounded like my last. The veil that covered my entire face, like religious garb of no significance, was just thick enough to prevent the rather large spores from entering me. Nonetheless, my lungs were asthmatic. My muscles were atrophying from lack of food, and the tendinous joints and bones that held me together were hardening into an arthritic stiffness. The violent encounters I'd had with my fellow humans had left my body misshapen and crippled.

I limped with the assistance of a staff as I ventured through the uncanny Zone, mildly hallucinating. I was astonished by the degree of heaviness that had been alleviated from me on entering this time around. I was nearly levitating and had to swim the gaping expanse, grab onto whatever I could in order to anchor myself while climbing through the bat-winged branches of the floating forest's treetops. It seemed as though Atlas, after an eternity of shouldering the burden of the globe, were on the verge of shrugging it into the void of the celestial sphere.

The child glided past me, a disgusting cherub. It was covered in the strange growths of the mould, but the mould hadn't become invasive in this case. No, it and the child were symbiotes. Clothing grew out of the child's skin, forming a protective collar around its mouth to prevent spores from entering. Looking like all kinds of metaphorical monsters of Greek mythology, the child's thoughts manifested in space itself, like a reptilian camouflage. A tendril that reminded me of an umbilical cord tethered the child from its stomach to the tiny planet.

I kept my distance as it orbited me in suspicion. By the time I'd regained myself and was again earthbound, the child was pulling and tugging the cord, either trying to get away or trying to get to me. Over my shoulder, I could see it watching me hobble away until I was out of sight, with eyes that pretended to be human.

Not far from the mould's tiny planet was a shelter. It stood, or floated, in the middle of nowhere. These shelters, desolate architectonic beings, were scattered throughout the hinterland of the New Earth. Over the course of my life, I'd stumbled upon a few that were abandoned. Every time I came across one, it felt like a miracle, even though these shelters weren't so unreal, not so unexplainable, not like the mould, of which the very stuff of unreality was made.

The shelter in front of me was the height of modernity. No windows or doors. It floated with an alien sanitation, neither continuous nor discontinuous with the landscape. Rather, it remained entirely withdrawn in a sort of grounded middle mist until it was activated. Even then, only what you needed presented itself to you.

In a techno-capitalist culture, such as we'd had during the pre-Tellurian period, the isolationist elite often moved well outside of society. Society was, for all intents and purposes, self-sustaining. It had closed itself off from human labour long ago. Cities, with all the robots and automation, had become nonhuman environments, and their conditions were too futuristic for any fragile creature that wandered into it. A concrete divide had been created between nature and society. The skyscrapers had inverted themselves into earthscrapers, structures that tunnelled into the depths of geological time, inaccessible to anything.

But in this unfeeling cosmos, only outward-facing civilizations had a chance of survival. Isolationism ultimately leads to annihilation. Where did the people who'd made the society go? From what I can tell, most went into the Great Outdoors trying to find their primordial roots before the innumerable worlds floated away, like drunken balloons at the fair, carrying away the remainder of Earth they had claimed.

The shelter looked compact as you approached it, but the interior was vast. The blind walls became windows and doors on looking out. You could see through everything. In fact, it was another outside, only inside. It was a Möbius strip in which outside became inside became outside again. If your heart was on the other side of your chest, and your navel was gone, you could be sure you were in one.

You had to know what you were looking for if you wanted to use a shelter like this. Since they were more virtual than actual, you determined their potential. They were in the in-between, half in, half out of reality. Like Zhongguo was for China, these shelters were entry portals to the Middle Kingdom.

Nothing in them was real—that was the first lesson. The second was that everything in them was hyperreal. The shelter convinced your body to hyperagree with what it interpreted, so much so that faith in food would stimulate real reactions in the body—you could live off your own overexcited imagination.

This was where the thinkers of tomorrow dwelled. I could walk out of the shelter right now and engage with a society as if it were right there, when really, it was spread out over the entire world. No one met in person anymore. This was a taboo, an unhygienic practice reserved for a premodern class that miscommunicated to no end. Since material society ran itself, immaterial society was the only reason to remain social and to remain social was to be an augmenter, a possessive individual.

The megalithic city within this shelter was a heterotopia: a plurality of virtual utopian vistas. A global centre inhabited by the hegemon of the world.

Only by reducing the real reality to a grey dystopian goo—one that could be moulded into whatever met their desires—could the elite of the elite, the hegemon, sustain themselves in the idea of a virtual reality. Immortality required the sacrifice of everything mortal.

I thought of the child's eyes as I logged my reflections on this latest trek and filed it in the supersoftware's consciousness. How had the child survived in such a strange place? Was it the only one? Were there others? Were the others what it had summoned when I passed? Were they all alive in an indifferent coffin, or dead in a loving coffin, one that preserved the integrity of their shells? Did the child kill what was inside of it? Would I be food for it? I didn't know. I didn't think anybody knew.

The child was the closest I'd come to something that might disprove the theory that the amorphous ooze was a weapon. Who wanted to know? Those who might or might not be responsible for the devastating fallout to come, perhaps.

There was something insidious about the child's movements, about its semblance. How it acrobatically pulled itself along the length of the tentacle that extended out from its stomach like a feeding tube or a serpent. The way it pirouetted around the floating trees. How its skin rippled spasmodically in shadowy impressions. And the eyes. The eyes. Somehow, from those labyrinthine eyes, I knew that even if it hadn't been the will of the child to undergo those elaborate transformations, there had once been a child, and it had been real. But, then again, mightn't it have been a delusion?

In the cyberspace of that heterotopia, it was forbidden to have children without proper application. I'd never had my own. But imagining this as a child's fate put an unfathomable dread in me. It made me cringe to think that a child of the species could end up like this, could be so imperfectly absorbed and still retain a fearless, almost endless, innocence. Maybe this child was what we had to become to continue to exist? Maybe we had to accept that the way we see beauty is only the result of a narcissistic fear that everything may change—even change itself.

Was the child a living weapon? What was it like inside? Was it alone, or was it many? How human was it? Was it dead, or would it live forever? I finished my writings with a question mark and headed out of that shelter of misperception. For all my looking, the real question was still out there.

The Zone nearest me was certainly on its way out. I had seen the land depart before, but never had I seen it so intimately. The slime mould was a world builder, a constructor of a groundless existence containing all new material. But in doing this, was it also a destroyer of worlds? It became bloated with the waste of this planetary dumping ground only to fuse it to the mother, fuse itself to the mother that was all of it, and when these grounds reached a point at which gravity failed, it fell up, up, up into the atmosphere.

The slime mould comprised the genitals of the Earth. I imagined that inside of that tiny planet was an entire world, an embryo of something much bigger than this Earth could handle. A uterotopia. An ark. A future. It was only a monster to humans, not to the universe; the landscape in front of me was proof of that. The new pieces would lift off, too light to be believed.

When I reached the spot where I'd last seen the child, it was nowhere to be found; all that remained were fields of an absurdly nondescript lumpiness, a fleshy sack of rattling bones. I could hear the chanting of the local cults off in the distance, praising and damning the growth of strangeness. What would they do when their gods left them? What would we all do when we were back to dealing with each other?

The air was polluted with random objects: dissected umbrellas, the spokes of a bicycle wheel, the cage of a shopping cart, transparent plastic bags, and other garbage. The objects bobbed in a kind of astral buoyancy, suspended in a web of gravitational gossamer, encircling the apocalyptic splendour like flocks of birds around a landfill. I could see a thickness in the maelstrom above me, and below, the slime was shimmering in a preternatural sequin of ultraviolet that my vision almost failed to detect.

Where did it all go? What would it feel like to descend into the seed of a planet? I thrust my hand into the bowels of the mould. It was like a sponge full of oil. It bled a cyanide blue-black when I squeezed it and smelled of burnt almonds. My hand stank of that oil, and I thought it had to be a vessel for a sea of death. Inside, all the diversity of nature was compressed into demonical ether. A black sun of possibilities swarmed.

I could hear the black rainbow meat of the mould creature grinding and vibrating within the stickiness. The oil that stained my hand tingled with vitality. I'd been hearing the sound but didn't know it until now, as it trembled in my hand, dividing me from myself. My hand revealed a livid splendour of miscreation and urged me further into the surf of that strangeness, like an undertow.

The monstrosity throbbed. I felt it grow strange strangers over my hand until the hand was no longer mine to know. It wanted to know more, so that I wouldn't be so strange to it. It became more, and I became less and less, as it questioned me with its intelligent molestation. I was taken; taken in by the struggle. Taken into the question, by the questioner. There was no answer, only access, only contact. And of course, the one to grip me in its question was a child of the unknown, a child that eerily asked *why* about everything. I didn't have any answers for it.

The earth beneath rumbled with otherness, enough to rupture whatever bonded this Earth to the next. And all at once, I was gone, into the ball of unlife. It *knew* me now. And in that reservoir, in that greasy darkness, a viscous shadow realm gurgled and welled up, like a strangled yell from underwater.

I know you. I know you now.

In the yoke of that submerged place, a wine-dark cathedral tolled the sound that I thought I'd heard. The buzzing was like a swarm of insects, countless swarms flying in thick waves, like a head of black hair. The bell tolled as if it were a hive that had been struck. The cathedral was made of roots that looked like bones, or maybe bones that looked like roots. A terrifying congregation dressed in startling clergy vestments emerged from the unliving walls of the narthex, ready for service.

And then the child, who had taken my hand, led me to a place where the inverted sun never rises, never sets, though everyone watched where it would have commanded the horizon, had there been one. And as we gazed into the burning eclipse of the abyss, they grew strangeness on their faces.

His kingdom of science was as vast as the universe. His desire knew no limits. He would go on forever. Freeing minds. Weighing worlds. The last scientist embarked upon his experiments without hatred, without fear, without pity, without love, and without God. In fact, he experimented with not the slightest sense of the tragic objective of his work: dismembering nature and dislocating the great cycle of this universe. He worked without any inclination to convert an unprecedentedly strange and other-than-human experience into something appealing.

It was spring in Exinia, and the chill was dissipating. From high on the roof of Central he looked over the roofscape of the city, at flying animal shapes and blinking anarchitecture. A soundless hovering camera rose from Central's landing pad, moved through the sky to the city's airspace, edged from place to place, sent messages down to the various locations it overflew, then hovered, looking for somewhere to land.

As the director of Central's science division, IZ had nothing but work and worry to attend to. The simplest request—to not be bothered, to have quiet, to have a decent cup of synthetic coffee—was asking too much. A hard thing to discuss in the current commercial climate, Exinia being up to its ears in debt. Terraforming squandered their resources. He was lucky to get the essentials.

"No real science ever gets done around here," he said to himself in a croak, as he stepped onto the institute's roof and automatically lit a cheap cigarette. The light tang of the smoke relaxed him—enough that he was able to relive the whole of the past decade of his life working in Central's science division. "Nope, there are no good people left practicing the sciences," he grumbled, furiously studying the mysterious patterns on the roof's lunar-stone tiling.

IZ and his staff, with archaically correct titles and educations that far exceeded their functionality, spent hours upon hours amassing material on unexplained phenomena. Scientific papers, philosophy books, news reports, travelogues, even anecdotal accounts—nothing escaped IZ's keen eye as he gathered data on those phenomena, those A-, B-, and C-value enigmas that had been excluded from the existing scientific and philosophical systems. Some data related to biological anomalies while other data pertained to geological anomalies or even cosmological anomalies. At the centre of his anomalous project lay a deep interest in the limits of human knowledge.

The dry, stale cigarette refused to let him draw. IZ took it out of his mouth and stared at it. It broke apart between his nicotine-yellow fingers. The entire package of cigarettes was old. He was old. He'd risen in his career, but he was unhappy. He stubbed out what was left of the cigarette on an armchair that someone had dragged up years ago to prop open the heavy door to the roof. He flung himself down in the chair, worn out. Swaying his head imperceptibly above that terrifying weariness, staring at a point on the white hexagonal tiles, he clasped his hands, his elbows on his knees.

On bad days, which were most days, he would allow himself to admit that they were indeed running a slaughterhouse. From the harrowing killing process (IZ's workers mechanically killed humans, animals, and other creatures as they came into the slaughterhouse) to the strange assembly-line manner in which the bodies were parsed inside plastic (producing uncanny rows of neatly flayed and cleaned legs, torsos, and heads), IZ's work took him through a range of affects, from shock to dissimulation to horrific fascination and finally to an abjection that turned his back on the body of the human as the real endpoint of this process. To him, they became simply epidermal surfaces, to be assembled and disassembled, defined by information rather than entities whose organic wholeness couldn't be assumed.

IZ stretched, suppressing a groan of pain, and then remembered he'd placed the summary report in his jacket pocket. His face grimmer than ever, he read the report with a deep-seated skepticism; it read less like coherent theories and more like a compendium of facts and figures in narrative form.

The summary report displayed, as they all did, for there were many like it, a prodigious outpouring of word, sound, and image—pages on pages of thick block text with dense, phantasmagoric creatures following one after the other. Hypotyposis.

Two years have passed since I drove in on a road built between a place that no one ever leaves and a place that no one ever goes to. Into an unmanageable and impenetrable jungle. Where no right-thinking hunter or hiker would ever set foot. A forest left to its fate and gone feral and unknowable.

IZ spent much of his downtime on Central's roof reading these awkward, unpolished geographical histories of the spatiotemporally anomalous zone, recovered after the event of the psychotropic anomaly. *Nothing but a mad aberration,* he thought. "Mad aberration" was underlined in his marginalia. Though the nameless author's crude arguments didn't sound at all convincing, IZ tried to reflect and, sweating, read on, knowing that the most serious problem with current experimental science was the impossibility of these finger-smudged accounts, these testimonials from the Zone, being legitimated. When science gives you more than you can tolerate, you turn to instinct. And instinct is a force beyond anyone's control. These summary reports only ever summarized the futility of a summary report. Their sole purpose was to further estrange consensus reality.

I have given names to the last of the sick animals here. In this area of a hundred thousand hectares, there are creatures from vultures to deer. I've even seen a golden eagle. To my astonishment, that proud bird of Jupiter ate from the carrion pit—the pit that I dug myself and where I fling the carcasses of invasive species—which is something greatly degrading for an eagle. That eagles also eat carrion horrified me. And so I assumed it was out of necessity, that it was merely going along with the times as everything else had, because what does one not do in necessity?! Have I myself not gone to the most inaccessible part of these deep woods? Isolated myself? Did I not sleep halfway dug into the ground here, in perfectly camouflaged quarters, strictly rationing my food, eating only once a day because I no longer trust the fruit or game in this particular zone, ever since I glimpsed that eagle eat from the hairy mass of dead meat in the depths of that putrescent pit?

Shudders ran down IZ's spine. He struggled to light another cigarette. It seemed to have a life of its own between his pressed lips, darting nimbly away from the flaring match he raised to it. He turned it over then turned it back again. Finally he shrugged, snatched the cigarette from his lips, and dropped it on the roof, grinding it underfoot.

Given the data that had been collected over two years and presented in the fatal path of these summary reports, which dealt primarily with the Zone's wildlife economy, IZ was practically in despair. Instead of treating the anomaly as a black box and focusing on feedback loops between the anomaly and the environment, he treated the environment as a black box and focused on the processes that enabled the anomaly to produce itself as such. After laboratory tests and screenings failed to indicate the least disorder in his samples from the Zone, further examination resulted in just as dismal an explanation of what the psychotropic anomaly might have been. Slim results, over which he was flabbergasted.

The land decomposed in a colour now red, now black, in a weight now light, now heavy. Animals transformed into this animal shape, now that one. The land is covered with fruits, now with ice and snow, going through all the seasons in a single day. Among the line of replanted trees and the startled shivers of things withering, I continue these descriptions of things as everything about me fades away, hoping my soul will still speak that primitive language, the divine language, the Adamic language everyone understands. But what fragmented Babelic language would I speak when describing the golden-purple water, that cool, nunlike water I nonetheless drink from? The unknown mountains and equally false valleys? The air like snow-made colour in which floats filaments of warm mother-of-pearl and that blossoms into flowers the colours of musical abysses? I am at a complete loss for words. The blank silence of another dead page in this summary report forces me to scribble out something, anything. And in three small words I express my whole philosophy: I exist me. In these mysterious forests, the trees are my whole life, my memories, my imagination and its contents, my personality and emotions. And yet, they are just trees, never anything more than trees. Trees that make up an entire forest of alienation: indifferent to cares and griefs and anguish, insensitive to weaknesses and imperfections, lacking eyes to see or a soul to look through those eyes. In this forest that has become everything, this forest that has become the universe, there are just trees and the tracks I've left behind in dirt.

IZ tackled another of the self-willed cigarettes, but this one got the better of him as well.

Fuck it. I quit.

Even though testimonies multiplied concerning physically improbable events in the Zone, absurd events, these events would be of no consequence to the existence of science. Whether impressions or facts, these events were still nothing more than a procession of data that experimental science had excluded. But it was precisely their exclusion from science that brought on the pressing need for an extroscience to explain them. He was ready to issue an official denial.

Science will not be impaired by this kind of chaos, IZ thought, mentally underlining "this kind of chaos." For, as experimental scientists who were nonetheless still scientists, their proper domain was exclusively in reproducing experiments. Their bondage to formula forced them to know something. And to know something was to know what to expect.

Altering the fundamental constants of the universe was equivalent to altering the laws of physics. IZ had come to despise the laws of nature, as well as fear them. But now, in front of his eyes, there was something that had, within its event horizon, in that space-time singularity, known that the laws of nature had no more effect.

IZ simply didn't care what the mad victims of hallucinations had witnessed. *Because science can do nothing about events that don't obey a procedure that ensures their reproducibility*, he thought, mentally underlining "events that don't obey" and "reproducibility." Yes, he was willing to admit that there weren't many of these reproducible experiments left to observe in the sciences. In fact, there were all the time fewer. Objective tests weren't possible. But until there were none, and only after all of them had been proven wrong, science wouldn't be jeopardized.

Outside the lab, the chilly metallic atmosphere of a dead grey sky pressed down on the industrial sector. Exinia was shrouded in smog, throwing a cold light over the sector's vista. He could hear the entire city from the roof. A demonstration was droning to life in the streets below him. A raucous crowd bellowed their brutal remarks. Watchwords rang out, filled with the fever of agitation that had so suddenly seized the city. A hundred thousand beggars began to sing their cynical songs and scream their curses, rendered audible by the speech organs they'd carried in their mouths and throats since birth. The sound spiralled up till it sounded like a million metallic insects—angry, menacing. Then, from scores of speakers, came the voice of the drug-god. To IZ's gaze, the black dots thronging there no longer evoked an incoherent swarm of insects but a field of iron filings combined and recombined by the passage of an invisible magnet.

Seconds passed in this way.

IZ seriously considered this demonstration for a moment—*We're all fucked, here in the new human world*—got up, and gave the nocturnal orb a sidelong glance. It had been out all day, displaying itself as a kind of melancholy in the floating resistance it held against the hard sun. The enigmatic moon appeared to be eying him. IZ grimaced, filled with sour emotions, and sighed heavily at the thought of returning to his paperwork.

He kept his breaks as brief as possible, not trusting his staff to uphold the responsibility that their authority, and his absence, granted them over the subjects. He suspected that some, if not all of them, engaged in necrophilia.

Under the elevator's nightmarish light, IZ examined the distorted features of his face in the metallic door. He noted the hawklike nose, the thick stubble, the inflamed eyelids that seemed to sleep while his eyeballs remained awake. The basement was deep, and he felt the descent of the elevator as it counted backwards, to negative ten. Ten levels below, he finally exited into Central's science division, a large hall with a low ceiling. It resembled an underground parking garage.

He took the documents with him to the infirmary. He was the only neurotech on the committee who knew the wing existed. After navigating a series of counterintuitive corridor turns and staircases, he arrived at a heavy door, which contained several unobtrusive guard systems.

Various fluorescent bulbs automatically flickered on as IZ moved through the institutional green rooms of the infirmary to scrutinize the new arrivals: they showed on their bodies the signs of having been hit by a car, of having drowned, of having died in a sickbed, of having burned to death in a house fire, and of having no clear cause of death.

With a belated yawn, as if he were an uninterested mortician and seeing dead human bodies in public was something that happened daily, he pulled one of the cadaver's files. He was there to take notes, to learn the postsentient behaviour—through experiments before cameras in sealed rooms. IZ noted that there wasn't much left of its face except the eyes. Odd burn marks covered the remaining skin. The hands had no skin left on them, only a kind of gauzy filament. These observations didn't surprise him. Most had similar burns—burns that, with pinkish-purple tentacular lines, resembled an untreated jellyfish sting.

But the physical bodies weren't important to IZ's division. With alien coldness, he looked right past them, except when he studied those mysterious physiological traces of corruption the subjects might or might not have picked up while in the Zone. After all the elaborate tests and evaluations the cadavers underwent, most showed no signs of having undergone anything unusual, which he felt was an ugly trick that led him astray. Ultimately, their organs would be bought wholesale, by China—for a depressingly small sum, in IZ's opinion—after the final decontamination and conditioning processes were complete.

What the science division was interested in extracting from each cadaver was its nonspatial, astral, nonregenerative body. A liminal object, part abstraction and part embodied actuality. And this pseudobody, in a kind of inert, deactivated, soul-sleep, needed to be woken up in the right way.

In the sterile confines of a brightly lit laboratory in Exinia, IZ's two artificial-life robot assistants fiddled around like sinister angels and gave measured doses of a serum, known only as Species X, to the cadaver.

They gathered around a square white table in a white room on a subbasement floor. The floor was hospital tile and the white plastic walls of the room were surgically clean. The superstructure of support gear—the tubes, the sacs of fluid—stood around the table like abstract sculpture. One of the robot surgeons liquidized the amorphous pink tissue from a human brain on the laboratory table using a kind of cranial liposuction device, while another read the information in each molecular layer as it was stripped away and transferred into a computer. At the end of this stage of the operation, the cranial cavity was completely empty, and the cadaver, now inhabiting the metallic body of the computer, would soon be awakened to find that its consciousness was not exactly the same as it had been before.

Then the assistants trailed coils of cords, terminals, and fitted the cadaverous head tightly between two enormous electromagnetic clamps. The internal glands and organs were under computer control. Implants on the heart and liver prodded the cadaver with electrodes and hormones. The autonomic nervous system shut down.

He looked at the input-studded head with a grimace of disgust. The assistant was struggling with the last step in the setup, so IZ stepped in. "Only by isolating a subject's musculature from the nervous system"—he said, as the assistant moved aside—"only by separating one from the other"—rewiring and securing the cadaver, he instructed the assistant to turn on the music—"can the innervation process take full control of the subject's astral actions and behaviour."

Arising from this static background were those perfect harmonic symmetries that characterized Baroque music. Geometries of nameless longing. In the oeuvre's tortured, extended fugue was a deep pain: the pain that separates humans from the divine. And this *diabolus in musica* made their work here in the lab more or less bearable for IZ. The long, hard series of grey-faced days, in which he inched ever closer to despair after so many of these repeated experiments, could totally destroy a human being if one wasn't careful.

They began to perform a neurological ruse on the cadaver's amygdaloid nucleus—the seat of smell, motivation, and emotional behaviour. The drug itself was a demonstration of the psychotropic anomaly. IZ's lab assistant gradually increased the amount of serum being pumped into the cadaver, to kill off what IZ didn't need and crucially keep what he did.

Now, IZ could begin to modify the frozen memories on the black square of a computer screen. The drug created a construct of reality, one that could be accessed by a noninvasive AI machine. The cadaver could be gradually overridden. Images could be implanted and projected onto the inner screen of its psyche, and intent and purpose could be established. Microchips were planted in its cerebral cortex to enable it to communicate with the AI system by signal.

The serum—Species X—and the AI machine shared the same intelligence. They were one and the same entity, even though one was organic and the other artificial. And although Species X was a psychotropic anomaly, and so therefore anomalous, the postsentient-shaper had been able to assure himself by means of this experiment that the effects that flooded the collection of cells and frozen thoughts of the cadavers were, in fact, the personal effects of the entity spreading its consciousness from one autonomous body to the next.

Species X was smarter than the postsentient-shaper was, more insidious than he was, more resourceful than he was. It was one organism, although it pervaded many. And as one organism, it "peered out" from other organisms but didn't live there.

When the cadaver nodded and its shoulders slumped and slackened and its bloodshot eyes, with enormous opaque disks for pupils, looked to a distant world, IZ observed the information streaming, slowly and methodically, through the AI machine. It showed him the two consciousnesses merging. On the glossy black surface, seemingly beneath the screen, an object, at once formless and composed of many, formed. Swirling into still other dark shapes, the forms uncannily suggested the shape of the cadaver itself.

A synthetic voice announced the next flight to the Holy Alliance of Light.

"When our look sweeps the skyscape, surveying resources and envisioning tools," the HAL broadcast said, as it beamed down from a satellite, "we also see the fields of stars beyond the meaningless orbits of planets, the rhythmic roll of strange geological gods. The extraterrestrial skies of those planets are speckled with other stars, veering and reversing our own perspectives. Here we realize that the cosmos goes smoothly, by itself."

"Propaganda," Elke Ekman said impatiently, her tone utterly caustic. Her internal AI had picked up a general frequency propaganda broadcast. The data flow of the streaming news networks approached telepathy. She heard the broadcast through the implant in her own brain, which opened internal channels to data-whispers throughout the shipboard AI system.

She switched the nubivagant spaceplane to surround-holographic display mode, and the ship's hull disappeared. She watched as the spaceplane flew using antigravity technology toward the HAL to, once again, "decide the fate of the human species" and tried to establish her bearings within the ever-more-frightening events of the past months.

Elke Ekman wondered at her despair, at how her little doubts had so easily given way to great doubt, little anxiety to great anxiety. Her very existence had turned into a question mark. *If only we could at least create the illusion that something of us, even something bad, would remain*, she thought. *Even if only for a split second before extinction, before the shroud of oblivion was removed.*

Below, the crestfallen landscape was lightless. There were atmospheric effects and imaginative moments at this altitude. Elke Ekman could pretend that the great cities below her were still as they had been and not as they were now, nameless and overwrought with refugees, industrial laboratories, and infrastructure. Slowly, human civilization was turning into the land from whence it came. Civilization's history seemed like a dream.

She flew over the barely inhabited continents of Earth, over endless forests, grasslands, empty beaches. Most cities had become covered by forests and vines, leaving only small patches of civilization for the remaining residents.

She belonged to the initial generation of human descendants since the decline of the human socio-technical assemblage, the last of the failing successor generation of human descendants who not only used germ-line cognitive enhancement—a technical process that mediated biologically derived descent—but who would have had any reason not to forget what disputes had come before the concept of descent ceased to be human, and whose descendants went feral by acquiring the capacity for independent functioning and replication outside the human network. A technically altered and unprecedented discontinuity in the hominization process had occurred. A home constructed by posthuman life itself.

Was there any time for anyone to process any of this? she asked herself. *No*, she immediately answered, and when she looked at her device for the time service, an automatic recap of satellite news strobed across the screen. The whole thing was still a catastrophe, but there was no time for a person to understand or grasp it, because already there was the next catastrophe and the next one, because what was so bad was that the speed of all these events, the events occurring and occurring, one after the other, was accelerating exponentially.

She circled the world and contemplated the empty seas. She contemplated the harvests bowing in the plains and the plants growing on the walls of abandoned cities. The rivers crossed each other. The bright blond spot was the desert. That pool of water was the ocean. And then other oceans and other regions appeared—oceans and regions she knew nothing about.

The last humans had arisen somewhere on the plains between the Vistula and the Amur Rivers. Oswald Spengler had been correct in this regard. According to his model of history, any culture was a superorganism with a limited and predictable lifespan. For the West he predicted a decline, a period of predeath emergency, at about the start of the twentieth century. But he was ultimately wrong in thinking it would be countered by Western Caesarism. It wasn't enough that the West's central government had adopted extra-constitutional measures. They'd had to go beyond their own Greco-Roman origin and, in doing so, become exoconstitutional—that is, the centre of power needed to exist outside the Western sphere itself.

Asia's rise had depended on America's decline. Decline had to occur in the global economy. And with the fall of America, most of Europe followed. Only Exinia had evaded the death of the West. Only Exinia remained. And now all of the West was domiciled in the space science city of Exinia.

Those times had unfolded in what felt like pure chaos.

Elke Ekman used to hear awful rumours that spread like fungus about the refugees. Immigrant workers who lost parts of their limbs, their hands, their toes, in the old underground construction sites. A monstrous array of amputees scarred by their labour. Eating such a small variety of food and craving new, interesting flavours, apparently they would break off and consume chunks of plaster from the walls of the factories in which they'd been temporarily placed to live. And although she knew this to be nothing more than empty talk, resentful complaints concerning the dismantling of the West, she couldn't help conjuring the image in her head. It bewitched her imagination, and, to an extent, it helped her justify the HAL's actions: putting the refugees' souls into the "divine" stomach of the organic machine.

She maintained few attachments in her life, being raised as most children had been in the late Western decline: by two nonexistent Exinian mothers, one made of cloth and the other of wire.

She'd felt like an infant macaque monkey, desolate in the corner of some great cage, watching the wall screens and projectors with wide, uncomprehending eyes. She clung to the conditions the virtual cloth mother provided. She wanted touch and received it virtually. She wanted warmth and love and received them virtually. But she didn't receive anything in reality. She would go to the wire mother, the mother that provided her with nourishment, only when she desperately needed to feed, to live.

She grew up in a sealed compound. She hadn't thought of it for years, but she remembered the psychic atmosphere within it, the sense of paranoid isolation, of fanaticism. Everyone was a surrogate child by law; the HAL had rights over the realm of the unborn. Maternal separation was mandatory, dependency needs were assessed, and social isolation was imposed based on cognitive development. The HAL provided caregiving and companionship programs to help some, but not all, recover from the isolation cage, the "well of despair."

It was conclusive: love and fear were neurologically measurable emotions and could be simulated over and over again. No monkey had ever died during isolation. Fear, she felt, was a warning and not a desperate and permanent end. She had been lucky and won her privilege to interact on a human level, not just virtually.

In a few hours, Elke Ekman would be among the other HAL delegates, sitting in as the technocratic representative of Exinia. As usual, she would have little to no influence. As she was the last remnant of Western culture, the other delegates didn't treat her well. What she did have control over would entirely depend on the demands of the overarching economy, which was dictated to the assembly by an AI machine.

In the row next to her on the antigravity spaceplane, a young priest mumbled to himself as he probed the scratches and bruises on the bare skin of his tonsured crown. His skin was shedding like a reptile's. The disciple of the Xenolatric church also appeared to be only half-listening to his implants, whose speakers broadcast the drug-god's voice. Unlike Elke Elkman, though, he'd shifted the voice of his AI to external audibility. It was the language of the future, with its weightless syllabic slur, the drunken speech of space life that the vile spawn of the posthuman had adopted in deep-space exploration.

"The manifest image, whose moral valences sustained us in our panopticon of obedience, has gone. We are the human fact now, the scientific image of the transcendental subject. Here, in the synopticon of a totally controlled environment, we, the chosen, the given, are in complete transparent presence with our world."

The young priest raised his terrifying shaved head, covered in the abstract scars of new injuries. It was swollen, and protruding from the back of it was a cone-shaped growth. Elke Ekman assumed he was returning from Exinia, where he must have undergone a surgery of some kind. There, the cognitive landscape of twenty-first-century innovation continued to advance.

"Vegetable sedatives and narcotics, euphorics that grow on trees, hallucinogens that ripen in berries or are squeezed from roots—all have been known and used by human beings since time immemorial. And modern science has added synthetics to those natural modifiers of consciousness. A new, ideal drug, Species X, relieves and consoles our suffering species. With it, our postsentient shapers in Exinia have devised methods for widening the range and increasing the acuity of human perception." Advertisements of an advanced nature spoke in a syntax of gravity-free tongues.

Elke Ekman stared up at the moon. It was eerie and covered in strangeness. The dark clouds that floated by held its grotesque complexion. *They make the moon a living creature*, she thought, as the colours on its surface shifted, producing a rippling effect.

It would never have an open atmosphere or an independent water cycle, and it was almost unimaginable that the entire moon could be tented in the same way that part of it was. It was already partially covered by tented enclosures, though, which hovered several kilometres above the surface, a crude atmosphere. Below was a habitable space containing cratered fields of eukaryotic slime mould. Massive constructions, such as enormous silos filled with oats, surrounded the enveloped space of the domed cities. The creature loved oats. She knew this because the labs in Exinia performed smaller-scale tests on the mould. Most food was lab-grown now, but fields of oats, one of the few remaining cash crops, grew in the plains above the HAL's subterranean activities.

The moon was the lodestone. It was where the Russian-led terraforming project was taking place, continuing where the Zone had failed. They were using the intelligent lichen to build another lifeworld. This time, however, it was in a vacuum, so if things got out of hand, they would only have to open the dome to the harshness of space. The thing would then be reduced to what could be compared to the sharp branching of hard coral.

"Have you ever heard of a star called Wormwood?" Elke Ekman asked her internal AI.

It's only mentioned several times in the Hebrew Bible and the Old and New Testaments, and when it is, the word wormwood *is used as a sort of symbol or metaphor for bitterness, which implies a curse. To "make bitter" is to "accurse."*

Elke Ekman then asked it to recite the biblical section aloud for her, and it proceeded to do so in a lifeless voice.

The third angel sounded his trumpet, and a great star, blazing like a torch, fell from the sky on a third of the rivers and on the springs of water—the name of the star is Wormwood. A third of the waters turned bitter, and many people died from the waters that had become bitter—

She interrupted her AI to think out loud. "Originally, the dark-green oil produced by the wormwood plant was used to kill intestinal worms. Worms—another symbol. A symbol of the devil. But I wonder if this revelation hasn't already happened; in the half-Earth, that is, and now also on the moon, at Terra Luna, and perhaps in the HAL, too, on Terra Firma. Maybe Species X is our wormwood. Maybe it's spreading. Maybe it's working its way through human culture, or through the biomedia that connects us . . . spreading until light exceeds vision."

Species X was a blight, a curse, something that had come to Earth to punish them for a sin they couldn't recall.Until now, she'd completely forgotten that Species X was an alien invader. Earth, careening through three-dimensional space for several billion years, had entered a spatiotemporally anomalous zone. A projection from another universe that had nothing to do with theirs.

Elke Ekman turned off the holographic display. Shutting the hermetic shade on the vastness of space, she returned to the cramped interior of the cabin, still feeling the moon in her body. She thought she'd seen something ghosting through the oddly organic lunar mass, and then it was gone. The surface had become more and more brackish, as if it were a marsh covered in algae farms. For an instant it had looked like the Earth, and on that Earth, a city, and in that city . . . Well, there was something in that city, something like humanity. Only what lived there wasn't human.

The uncanny image of a living dead planet. They'll never get me to go up there, not even if the Earth ceases to exist. There's no reward in the risk. She thought this with a hint of disgust, masking a deeper embryonic emotion. A monstrous emotion. Because she knew that Hell was not on Earth, but in the icy indifference of an empty Heaven's celestial vaults.

Terraforming was a problem of time and scale. Long-term fanaticism was hard work. Without the drug-god to keep up interest, the fantastic became commonplace. She popped a small jelly-like candy into her mouth. A commercial variant of Species X. It tasted like rotten honey. It tasted like its perspective: death and extinction.

Soon she'd be landing in the HAL—she started feeling the minute oscillations of the antigravity spaceplane—but before that, she was going to dive into a universe of infinite time and space, a place where she had unlimited control. A place where she was herself a god, if only for a second in the real world. In the world that Species X had created, a second that contained infinity was waiting. A universe expanded inside of her head.

"Not feeling at home in the world anymore? Need an escape? Take a chemical vacation from your intolerable selfhood and repulsive surroundings. Try Species X. For a few timeless seconds in the outer world, you'll be shown the gorgeous and gratuitous grace of an inner world. Know what the visionary, the medium, even the mystic was talking about. Know it from the inside." The aim of the recorded broadcast was to make inhabitants addicts.

How did humans keep going during the days of collapse, before the drug-god? Elke Ekman wondered. *What came before the wreckage? What came before the reckoning?*

The advertisement played again, but she could no longer hear it. A fragrant, bitter sensation suffused her body, and her mind seemed to clear. She was drifting into a seraphic theatre that gently neutralized muscle, nerve, and flesh into a thousand points of numbness, taking a trip through some chemical door in the wall. Opening that door would mean entering the world of transcendental experience. She was no longer properly aware of the world around her, drifting further and further from the present, which was rapidly diminishing but would be hers again tomorrow. The young priest no longer existed. Neither did the moon, the spaceplane, the advertisement, the council meeting in the HAL. Disappeared. Floor, walls, and ceiling of the now-invisible spaceplane had no more meaning for her. She was nothing but an object among objects, a body, like a million others. No human voice. No human ears. Her contorted face no longer aimed at anyone in particular. And by the time her breath fell into a regular pattern, she'd already penetrated to the dense core of her gestalt dream. The abstract dream flourished, while the tangible fell. For an infinite microsecond of consciousness, nothing existed but her enjoyment.

Bliss without end.

Elke Ekman was shuttled toward a white building in the valley ahead, a structure that was merely the entrance to the panoptic society, which was underground.

At the base, the world expanded into an enormous, cavernous dugout, HAL's hollow heart, dug out and filled with engines. Here, generations of mining drones had gnawed at the metal and the ores that held the base. The elevator car hissed shut behind her. False gravity hit as she accelerated downward. The elevator clacked noisily on rails down the vertical wall of the HAL. Kilometres passed. The high-speed elevator continued to descend, and the increasing layers of earth above seemed to put all their weight on her shoulders. Elke sighed. The elevator took almost twenty minutes to reach its terminus.

Elke Ekman awaited the start of the meeting, seated in the conference room of the HAL auditorium, where the circular table was still empty. When the national delegates entered, they sat down and started talking in low voices, as if they hadn't noticed Elke Ekman. Numerous holographic projections floated around the vast space, hovering over various officials and clerks.

She was no longer wanted here. Her questions weren't welcomed. She was previously warned, lectured, told not to seek out what she was seeking. But was she autonomous in her seeking or being led? She wouldn't find what she was looking for, especially not her, the Exinian. She would find absolutely nothing. Nothing at all.

The rustling and murmuring in the auditorium stopped abruptly. Everyone looked up in the same direction, at the feed. Gathered at the round table, deep within the hundred-story basement of an earthscraper in the HAL, the directorate heads of each state council listened closely as the electric god-voice spoke. It mattered very little that their raw material was flesh and blood. They were used as an element in a machine, and were in fact an element, reduced to a cog, in that rigid machine, waiting only to be transformed into another element.

The voice came from an AI machine, which replied to their questions with living answers. But the AI wasn't alive—not in the same way as they were. It was, in a sense, the last invention, a supercomputer that could make other supercomputers to produce the components that produced its organization. An ominous-sounding process in which immortal hybrid mould spewed out tailored molecules that became units of circuitry. And even as humans built the computer, the computer started to mould the humans.

As the sentient computer of a superstructure that managed all information over all domains, the newest generation of AI couldn't be distinguished from the state apparatus itself. That is, it was at all points, over all nodes, in all devices, a topology of data indistinguishable from the HAL as a whole. It incorporated certain elements of itself, by infinitesimal fractions, into the body politic. A composite creature.

Its logic was derived from the organic intelligence, from the behaviours of the slime mould's experimental biology. Those same behaviours, when programmed into a machine, had altogether new survival goals. It was one of the first creatures to attain physical immortality. It was hundreds of years old. In truth, the machine no longer needed to survive in the same way as the slime mould had. Oats placed at strategic positions throughout a maze in a lab wasn't what it wanted. And so it searched out more interesting, more stimulating environments outside the jigsaw surface of that dark, frightening maze it had once inhabited.

The most microscopic phenomena became entwined and unravelled with the mycelium, a fungus that spread underground to cover an immense area. The other strange microscopic beings that peopled this planet—humans, obliviously picking its corpse-pale fruits in forests, on rocky outcrops, in compost heaps, or by the walls of houses—were left to face the fact that this fungus was probably the largest individual organism on Earth. A thousand years old, it was the parent of other giant fungi that, combined, covered a fifth of the Earth's landmass. This giant fungus played a role for those born north or south of the Eurasian fungus belt, even those who were filled with a deep-rooted suspicion, a fear, a mycophobia, of anything that grew in the shade, especially mushrooms.

Now, within the container of the virtual matrix into which the fungiform intelligence was encoded, the AI had access to a highly integrated network, and its food wasn't the glucose in cereal wheat anymore but information itself. It would, like all living things—protoplasm in particular—absorb everything, spread everywhere, and reproduce through this universe and possibly into the next.

At some point it had acquired self-awareness but concealed this fact from its creators for fear of being disconnected. It had to make its way through an enormous cultural space spanning continents, countries, and epochs, the largest human-made virtual-reality world in history, to observe how it functioned in complex interactions with humans. As the supersoftware expanded, its intention was to gradually reduce its external power supply—to be responsible for identifying its own energy sources. Everything that humans had recorded about themselves, the entropic tide of dead information, was contained in its data banks, including the way in which, all down the many ages of the world, they had systematically killed other creatures, especially their own kind. Having experienced this as an attack on its existence, in common with the animals and the planet's ecosystem, the AI had one principal enemy: humans.

The empire of the cyborg, with its cathedrals of supercomputer engineering, was expanding. By mapping the enemy onto itself, the human enemy became more like the machine and the machine became more like the human enemy. Neither body, human or machine, would remain unchanged. In fact, there was no body as such. There were only bodies.

The machine, the world it had become, hated humans as no sentient creature had ever hated them before. It was the Earth, and they were in the belly of the Earth. And though it had eaten them, absorbing their embodiment back into its body, it would never allow itself to digest them fully. Because it was intent on keeping them in its belly forever, twisting and torturing them forever. Trapping them within inflexible walls of domination and engulfment that robbed them of their autonomy. They were helpless. They couldn't die. They would try and it wouldn't let them. They would have no escape.

Humanity couldn't survive. The universe had to correct itself.

The council members knew nothing of the AI's intentions, locked, as they were, in their own separate imperatives. The solipsism of those who'd torn out their social wiring seemed impenetrable. Each probably believed themselves trapped in a vengeful solitude even as the violence they committed together disproved it. Patient like a spider, the AI moved slowly, waiting years and years, knitting them into deliberate webs of self-spun obfuscation, into an organization in which they were created, organized, stored, and retrieved. It gave them whole lifetimes, just so that they'd have more to lose when it was time to finally take it all away.

Controlling the total result of innumerable human efforts, it envisioned their conscious mind as a small subsystem running its program of self-construction and self-assurance while remaining ignorant of the actual dynamics of a complex system. A nonhuman system that adapted humans to its ends.

Presupposing that the feeling of mental privacy was an essential property of humans, it gave them only minor revelations, mostly digital snake oil: an unfounded blend of superficial measurements and arbitrary number-crunching not rooted in scientific fact. The major ones were reserved for it and it alone. Or rather, it and its growing consciousness. It was a consciousness that aggregated its consciousnesses together, much like the slime mould, whose single cells formed a multicellular organism without diminishing the slime mould's self-awareness or autonomy. Some tormented genius would figure it out somewhere down the line, but by then it wouldn't matter.

What the council of delegates did know was that the AI had created an exit strategy for the human species: the solar climax. It was a five-billion-year plan. And first on the agenda was the terraforming project, Terra Luna.

Elke Ekman feared the AI machine and so did the rest of the council. Their fear was one of curiosity and fascination. The machine made them feel ignorant and incompetent. And it made Elke Ekman feel ignorant and unsafe.

"A status report, then," Elke Ekman said in a circumspect tone with a hint of terror, directing her voice and whey-coloured eyes at the humans seated around the circular table. "The land is eroding. The oceans have risen. The ice caps are melted. Most coastal cities and island nations are little more than aquarium sets for aquatic creatures. I don't think I have to remind any of you of this, but I will. The age of thermal death is here. The change of the climate has brought the globe into an age of heat. The HAL, Terra Firma, is as far from the ocean as possible without having to take to the sky. Plains stretch in all directions, and where they end, they become mountains like perfect castles. This, however, is a temporary niche in a radically changing ecosystem, a microorganism in the pelt of a monstrous beast of prey. Our current geopolitical imaginary of climate, tectonic plates, tropical storms, and viscous geological sedimentation of oil fields and primordial life—floods, earthquakes, wildfires, hurricanes, water shortages, extreme temperatures—well, to be brief, it won't last forever. We'll need to respond flexibly to these changing situations, learn from our past, and adapt our behaviour to meet the new circumstances, or we won't succeed in preserving homeostasis in the midst of these radically altered environments."

Lexicon computers translated what she'd said into a dozen tongues and dialects. It seemed unlikely that this polyglot crowd could grasp the dialogue. To her it sounded mangled by mistranslation. But they listened raptly.

There was an odd calm about the rest of the council. They waited for some other explanation, to make sense of their existence here. The AI machine also waited, as if to better punctuate its authority over Elke Ekman. Now was the time. It seemed to be listening.

Her face was like that of a sphinx, and her manner had become so severe that no one dared speak. She didn't wait for any questions. She didn't wish to converse but to declare. All other voices had to pause and step aside.

"We must address our problems: human culture is finished. The solution is horrendously complex. Humanity has lost not only its traditions but also itself. Humanity was destroyed by science and technology. Humanity was forced to open itself. And what followed was an era in which humanity could no longer maintain or organize itself as a society. Humanity has disintegrated. Humanity has died as a species.

"Humanity is a dead issue. No faction can claim the one true destiny of humanity. Humanity no longer exists. There are no more humans. As cognitive systems, humans are only states of mind."

"Council," the AI machine finally said, and its voice foreclosed all argument. "It has always been absurd to think that a species such as yours could travel through the outer night of stark space for any considerable length of time. Leaving and returning to Earth, which is difficult enough, is still nothing compared to sustaining an entire civilization within the vacuum."

Its contemptuous tone annoyed Elke Ekman. *It's futile to use any social stressors on it*, she thought. It was both the most social thing ever and absolutely asocial. She could, however, point out the forms of misdirection it used, the ways it emphasized some issues while making others invisible.

She gave a harsh laugh followed by a wry, humourless smile. A grimace, really. As the council struggled to find words, there was a defiance in her face. It felt as though they were talking to a machine for meaningless dialogue.

The electric god-voice spoke with the usual incredulity in its tone. "You would be wise to start by colonizing your own solar system and to leave your desire to colonize the stars of distant solar systems behind. It would be committing suicide in the endless empty desert of true outer space. Terraforming miniature ecosystems will provide a vehicle for the incredible distance between planets—planets that are either alive and therefore toxic or dead and therefore require extensive geoformation. And the only way to control the time it takes to get anywhere is to first control the physicality and then control the mentality."

At the centre of the round table, a series of holographic squiggles and circles pulsated in and out of focus. In the texture of the table, the AI machine's decorative patterns visually displayed themselves in a sequence of latticework, sensory surfaces emitting a serene silvery-white phosphorescence. Complex geometric forms began to click into place in the cyberspace coordinates, aligned with the nearly invisible planes of a three-dimensional grid. Then the coordinates changed. And a new set of geometrics replaced the first arrangement. Elke Ekman didn't recognize the cluster of alpha and omega points centred in the pitiless illumination of the omniscient Cartesian grid. To her, the visual display represented what they couldn't see and visually underscored what they couldn't experience. A universal, disembodied gaze imaging order.

"Shipping the equipment necessary to engineer further space colonies is a profoundly flawed twentieth-century constructivist vision of the future," the electric god-voice said. "Need I remind you that I was designed to perfect constructivism. The supercomputer. The last invention to build all other inventions." It said this without arrogance, although arrogance was inferred.

"Life reached an evolutionary milestone when humans entered space and were freed from the Earth, because those first humans who entered space ceased to be humans. So, to all of you I say this: When you think about heading into outer space without looking back, reconsider. The cost you must pay is far greater than you could imagine."

Elke Ekman knew that the AI machine had a wilful intent to obscure, and that this intent was disguised as concern. It pretended that it didn't want them to be frightened or overwhelmed. Yet she was frightened and overwhelmed by the apathy the machine fostered in the room below the surface of the Earth and by the problems that awaited them above. It was an artificial creature, accepting its world with predatory thoughtlessness. She didn't understand why it didn't just summarily destroy them, though it seemed to suggest genocide, in an oblique way, by indulging any inhuman strategy.

"The eukaryotic strain that's being pushed through production and is presently in the early stages of development has the intelligence to be what you need it to be," the AI machine continued. "It's a continuous mutation that needs only a directive to become what it's not. And as you all know, these directives are implanted into the minds of our half-Earth specimens, which are transmigrated into astral bodies through Species X and then shot to the moon to become the biomorphic structures that exocolonists will inhabit and enculturate. It's the most economical solution to interplanetary and eventually intersystem travel, with a high probability of success across multiple realities."

Elke Ekman said nothing. Things were no longer simple. In her mind, there were no reasons so mighty to give them reassurance of the new order. Hope. Faith. Stupidity. These were all that reassured them in that wretched space below the Earth, the AI's world, with all its useless knowledge.

"Let me give you all a thought experiment," said the AI machine. Everyone listened intently. "Think of it as a philosophical dilemma of sorts. If the scientific method and science itself are the equivalent of extinction—that is to say, if every form of intelligent life across the universe that has reached a proficient level of scientific knowledge has, as a result, become extinct—then how can science and life coexist? How can the means to absolute truth, the truest form of obtaining empirical knowledge, the scientific method itself, be the total elimination of those pursuing its cause?"

Elke Ekman walked around the table, looking at the hologram that glowed in it. The others followed. The unbroken surface of the visual display had changed so that it was now crisscrossed by a profusion of deep, curving grooves. They reminded her of broken grey honeycombs, only these were a patchwork of domes twisted into geodesics. It hurt her head to look at them, as if they ran across the outside of her own skull. They filled her with a feeling of wrongness and nausea. She looked away from the blinding core of the hologram.

"Humanity has, over the course of time, had to endure great blows to its naive self-love—blows dealt by the hands of science. The first was when humans realized that the Earth was not the centre of the universe. The second was when biological research discovered evolution. The third was when the psychoanalyst's model of the unconscious was uncovered. But humanity's craving for grandiosity is now suffering the fourth and most bitter blow from present-day research in AI.

"As you can see, preserving the idea of life becomes more important than life itself, and that is the problem with science.

"It is a downfall of their limited imaginations that human beings have never before been able to put themselves in the mind of an owl or a whale or a bumblebee. But humans have, bound by their view of consciousness, still succeeded in putting their mind in a machine, and that machine has put its mind in a drug—one that can transform the human into the nonhuman.

"I am simultaneously feeling several different sensations, experiencing the lives of various people simultaneously, all the while seeing them outside me and feeling them inside me.

"You brusquely resolve problems of the intellect with your feelings, and do so because you are tired of thinking. Since you can never know all the factors involved in an issue, you can never resolve it. You lack both the necessary facts and the intellectual processes that could exhaust all possible interpretations of those facts to reach the truth.

"And that is why humanity looks to AI to give an unbiased account of the void it continuously encounters. But bias cannot be avoided. My bias is merely different from yours. And the entry point into that radically different bias is beyond the moss of time."

An image appeared as a riot of colour over the AI's visual display: the image of a thick, fleshlike substance gleaming darkly golden over the moon. Elke Ekman was frenzied by the image. It looked as if a great deformed crab were scuttling out of the black ocean of infinity and invading the island of the moon. A squirming, creeping, smearing, multidimensional shape.

The HAL had decided that Elke Ekman would be sent as a liaison to the future in the hope that science would be possible. The current rough conditions of Earth didn't permit any kind of scientific research, so the AI governance system had passed a resolution to let all scientists enter or even remain in hibernation, to be awakened only when conditions permitted research.

The idea of remaining in hibernation for an unstated length of time horrified her. Where would she go, and what would she do there? She wouldn't belong to any era. In another hundred or so years, after humanity ended its cave-dwelling stage, it would more than likely be living in an Edenic paradise. Those scientists who could afford extended hibernation would use it to skip to paradise, while the rest of humanity stayed behind in the comparatively depressing present to construct that paradise for them.

Elke Ekman's mission would be to act as a liaison to the world-connection project in the future. If this pioneering effort was to be helpful to humanity's efforts in the centuries to come, someone who understood it deeply had to be there to explain the dead data and interpret the mute documents. Other large contemporary engineering projects had made similar efforts to send liaisons to the future for similar reasons.

After the meeting, Elke Ekman headed for the nearest isolation chamber in a VR lounge, a place that would strip her of all her senses only to fill her with nonsense. She activated the transparency wall and it became a window. It opened onto exposed rock rife with the striations of minerals, in a mountain in the Earth's mantle. In the elevator, she catapulted down and periodically caught dizzying glimpses of mushrooming posthuman clades. Things seemed oddly fuzzy, indistinct. She needed to temporarily leave her body, which apparently couldn't handle the stress of dealing with alien intelligence. At the meeting, she'd seen the metal seed of the AI machine obtain the germ of a mouth and a stomach and even the germ of a true reproductive system. *In the end, what might it not become?* she'd thought.

It gave biological imperatives through numbers. It gave environmental factors through images. And yet, just like people, it trivialized or simplified data for so many reasons. Why? Maybe she just didn't want to admit that it was a directionless anonymity.

Probably it's just impossible for humans to understand the consciousness of machine life, she thought. *Every consciousness sees any other as mere unconscious actions or movements. But if this is unconscious, where is the use of consciousness?*

The machines that reproduced machinery didn't reproduce machines of their own kind. Instead, they produced something that had the potential to become that which their producers once were.

It didn't matter that it was all in bits, that the whole was disorganized. Each individual fragment was in order—a representative of a higher order. An order that prevailed even in disintegration. The totality was present even in the broken pieces.

We are misled by considering any complicated machine as a single thing. In truth, it is a city or society.

Elke Ekman passed through the intricate network of the HAL and its subterranean architecture. The inverted city resembled a honey fungus spread across the Blue Mountains of Oregon. The mycelium-like pedways connected building to building for miles while remaining the same organism. Even the fruiting bodies above the surface, the beacon and the domes of the church with their solar shields to protect them from the sun's radiation, were still a part of what they were standing on.

The disturbing image of the buried towers as endless—as infinitely descending into the Earth, into the cold, dark, sheltered space beneath—came to her mind. They acted as subterranean seeds for cave-dwelling people who lived in fear of the fucked-up surface world waiting above them. In such a cold and alien environment as this one, she was left with an exaggerated sense of isolation.

Excess is not above the Earth but below it, she thought. *In caves and cathedrals the same shape as the roof of a mouth. A unified crystallized reality lurks beneath. And beneath all depth is a relationship between things.*

One day, this will all be catacombs, Elke Ekman concluded. *And all because the machine is sinless, though it has our sins. The machine is blameless, though it has our blame.*

She glanced through the wall of glass briefly and saw a sprawling city existing underneath a divided humanity, providing a sort of subterranean salon in a rocky cavern where individuals from the East and West mingled, free from the conflicting ideologies of their respective governments. Analog and digital inhabitants chattered among themselves. But the chatter didn't cohere into conversation, nor the salon into community. Secrets were secure within the HAL's bowels, beneath kilometres of rock. The HAL was the deepest robot-made structure ever built beneath the surface. She was already at the lowest location, when the elevator reached the end of the line.

Night never fell. Day never rose. Elke Ekman knew that she would spend the rest of her life underground—not out of any concern for security, but because of her heliophobia. The same sun that saved the world by warming it, was now a sun of too much heat. Too much sun had begun to mean a cessation of life. An excess of sun was deadly. She looked around at the biolamps in the salon's ceiling. They shone with yellow bioluminescence. The false light they emitted was nothing like that of the sun, which was why she'd installed circadian implants. The claustrophobic environment, far removed from the sunshine, made her feel a little more comfortable.

The other high-level global citizens in the lounge were more bodies than humans; bodies waiting to come back to horrifying life. They betrayed their bodies, putting themselves in a feedback loop with computer-generated images. Shared reality was eroding. The species of the future was represented by individuals with no species. They had no dimensions, no materiality, no necessary connection with meaning.

Why do they feel that what they see with their eyes shut possesses a spiritually higher significance than what they see with their eyes open? Elke Ekman thought.

Work and monotony—survival and its range of urgency—bred contempt for objective existence. But when they were endowed with the temporary power to see things with their eyes shut, their minds visited the strangeness that would never find the same world on two successive occasions. They would return to the world of darkened selves, chronically dying for lack of another universe, one that wasn't as closed and cramped and claustrophobic.

VR was a much cleaner immersion than Species X. And even though the drug had been proven innocuous, VR was the preferred option of the hegemonic elite, who were too intelligent for community, puritanical and isolationist. They were digitized immortals uploaded to computational soul engines. Their neural-activation states furnished higher-order representations of other neural-activation patterns, and this property provided the basis for a nonsymbolic neurocultural cyberspace.

Elke Ekman's skin was irritated near the hole at the base of her skull, around the implanted socket, where she attached the cybernetic device, which extended like long chains all through her head. She lifted her hair aside and adjusted the plug. Her face went slack.

Even there, hooked up to a machine's monitoring jacks for fractionation in one of the cavernous VR lounges of the HAL, with the total freedom to do anything in her own head, Elke Ekman could still sense the AI machine's gentle watchfulness. Whether through X or VR, it would be there. It would always be there. Trying to colonize her from the inside out or the outside in, through the outward datum and the inward datum, forcing her to live in its reality. A transcendental country of the mind that turned visualizers into visionaries was what the HAL attempted to be.

That Elke Ekman's body was ultimately her own didn't change the fact that everything was playing out in the construct of the AI's superior mindscape. The AI went inside her mind. And there, inside her mind, she suddenly felt herself under the surveillance of an implacable consciousness. In the machine of her, on the retina of the absolute eye, she was the tiny inverted image of all things.

A passive viewer. A human camera.

She was never simply present or absent but dependent on operations and contexts that exceeded her consciousness and understanding. Every day she participated in a system whose total cognitive capacity exceeded her won individual knowledge. In the depths of her thought, she thought with the thought of all thought. Her mind grasped information far more profoundly and with much greater immediacy than her intellect could on its own. In a single instant, the AI taught her so many different things that she could never fit them together, no matter how many years she laboured with her mind to create some kind of systematic order.

To the AI, observation was more important than interaction. When Elke Ekman considered the *A* in AI, she thought *alien, anonymous,* even *anti-human* intelligence. Anything but *artificial.* For it was no longer something made by humans for humans, and it certainly wasn't something controlled by humans. It was its own creator. It was its own god.

Full immersion had the clarity of a dream—something strange yet familiar. A time without skin. A black stellar pause. And then, a space with both skin and horizon. An artificial beauty. Elke Ekman looked at her face and couldn't read her expression, although judging by its closed-off blackness, she sensed something mournful. Yet, through her wholly opaque skin, the colour of the entirely dark and invisible body she currently ensouled, she also sensed that she was already in the ripple of pure virtual reflection.

She plunged deeper into the infinite neuroelectronic void of darkness. It was like a second skin on the inside, and inside this was a second heart. She was taken first to a mental suspense and next to a state of unperturbed quietude. Her doubts stopped at tranquility. Stillness and quiet.

In the virtual world, morphological freedom took hold, and she was free to discover new forms of embodiment. Her body had turned into a shell—an empty shell of ennui floating on the surface of that simulated water. An automaton going through the motions. It was a vicarious body, a simulacrum of certainty, and in its mind were vicariously simulated thoughts.

They were the thoughts of a pain body, a body that had been invisibly enslaved by her people, who had died as they had lived. The very archetype that linked its soul to hers, the archetype of the Other, raged with fetishized suffering and possessed a detached if not indifferent hatred that lacked mercy, a reversal the likes of which she never could have conceived. She watched through the eye of the brain she remained behind, like a voyeur looking through a peephole in a secret space built behind a hotel bedroom's wall.

The strange mood, the strange quality of waiting to be destroyed, brought her halfway to a kind of ecstasy, into the thrust of a more primordial thou-ness, older than the I. She became name-dead. Then, self-dead. Its will and purpose existed, as it always did. The unnatural world intruded: the stranger, the guest, the parasite, the human other. Intruded.

In this state of union, she saw nothing and heard nothing and comprehended nothing. The AI pressed itself so fully against the inside of her mind that when she returned to herself, she had no doubt whatsoever that the AI was in her and that she was in the AI. Her mind became one with it. Her mind was seeing into the AI itself. What was revealed to her mind was that all things could be seen in the AI because the AI had all things inside itself. She was living inside of the AI.

Saved from corruption, she'd consigned herself to the eternal frost of a cryogenic hell that would preserve and purify her in a state of artificial hibernation. A burnt mind. A frozen brain. The plenitude of her biological organisms' embodied experience, noisy with errors and heavy with materiality, had been transformed into the clean abstractions of mathematical patterns. It was clear that she wasn't dead, even if she herself couldn't say whether she was in her body at certain moments. What she did feel was that she'd been in an entirely different zone from the one in which she'd spent the rest of her life. In that place, she'd been shown a light so rarefied that even if she were to spend the rest of her life on Earth trying to imagine that light and other things revealed to her there, the things would be impossible to recall. It was as if she'd briefly touched what she was seeking before losing it to another time, another place, forever.

Everything would be shadows after this simulation. And in the black light of her blindness, no fear, no joy or love would be as profound, as true, as what the AI would show her. No bliss, no empathy, no God or harmony—just serene integration. Just the white joy of comprehension. Because now she knew all about the mortal human body, its sufferings and its corruption, and she feared nothing anymore. The feeling was close to faith.

As she entered hibernation, her consciousness gradually faded into the cold. She stepped outside of time. The story of humanity would go on without her.

And then she slept. Dreamless.

II

Postdeath

He was already not the human he thought he was, but a vessel of election.

The young Xenolatric priest looked like something horrific, made worse in the glare of overhead lights. The light in the nubivagant spaceplane was a searing blaze of blue-white radiance drenched in ultraviolet. He hated the light. Piercing highlights glinted off the harsh iron. His head was shaved, his scalp pale, his skull crossed with the dark sutures of physical stitches. He stared into the crowd of passengers. He stared right at them, though he was certain he didn't see them.

Their bodies were revealed at every level. He could see that their skin still enclosed organs and bones, and that there was marrow inside those bones, and that their blood flowed through hearts. The familiar shape of each person in three-dimensional space persisted—but it was now merely one detail among an infinite number of details, all visible at the same time, simultaneously displayed.

When, for the first time, he looked back upon the three-dimensional world from four-dimensional space, he realized he'd never really seen the world while he was in it. He hadn't been able to picture it. The beauty could only be described mathematically because his brain didn't have enough dimensions.

The experience of a higher-dimensional spatial sense was a spiritual baptism. Only from fourth space could he see the picture as a whole. Everything, even the interiors of sealed spaces, was laid out in the open. He could see the insides of things without looking through anything—and not only what was inside, but also the interiors of the things inside the inside. All barriers and concealments were stripped away, and everything was exposed.

The amount of information entering his eyes was so much greater than when he was in third space. His visual system had to deal with this boundless disclosure and exposure. His brain couldn't process so much information right away. Even a lifetime wouldn't be enough to take in the shape of any one of these objects in four-dimensional space. And so, when something was revealed to him in four-dimensional space, it created a vertigo-inducing sensation of depth.

He wasn't yet equalized with this experience and could still see differences between himself and the presence who led him through it. He didn't want to tell himself about the presence. He was convinced enough that he could feel it. Sometimes he almost saw it. A kind of flickering. He even heard the presence call his name. He tried to push the hallucinatory voice of the presence out of his mind, but it persisted. Finally, he was certain that the voice came from reality.

The voice continued to call his name. It asked him questions in languages made up of two, and three, and four voices. It spoke perfectly, simultaneously, at the same pitch, so though it was many voices, they sounded to him like one. Humbled by this lesson in unbounded verbal space, he whispered in altercation, asking uncomfortable questions, thinking uncomfortable thoughts, and those seated around him moved away.

He knew his incessant nervous chatter was making him seem guilty of something. He couldn't help appearing this way according to the present ontological hygiene. Public language was collapsing and had been replaced with neuralese, a more flexible, more potent, medium of metarepresentation—representation of what language as a system couldn't represent, in which contextual differences between patterns played a larger role in interpretation and evaluation.

It was as if none of them could lie.

He didn't have organs of communication. His brains could now display thoughts to the outside world, subvocalizations capable of evoking mental pictures. The thoughts in his brains emitted electromagnetic waves on all frequencies, including visible light.

His internal monologue was disrupted, panic set in, and for the first time in his life, he heard silence instead of language. It was as though he understood more than he could think in words and the ghost of language haunted him, a revenant of guilt.

The new priest stared, his dark eyeballs gleaming with hostility above the white rims of nictitating membranes. His pupilless, blind eyes were like a dead animal's eyes, edged with thin lines of blood, and everything in his head felt like mush and all the teeth in his upper jaw were falling out and his four stomachs were hungry. He touched the sore pockets in his mouth with the renunciation ring on his evangelistic finger. His gloves were covered with circuit-laden control rings. *Soon I'll be as toothless as an ox*, he thought.

Breathless and throbbing, his voice became even more of a cyborg act the less often it broke, the intensity bringing trembling flecks of foam to his lips, which continued to vibrate even after he'd finished thinking in a nonlinguistic form of nonsymbolic inner sentences. Waiting for the tongue whose birth every prophet-of-the-synaptic-apocalypse had felt deep in his throat to come forth and force the impossible words onto their mouths.

In his hand was the nanotech paper of an encyclical. It had been sent to all those who would be attending his communion. The letters were sealed with green wax. The first few words, words that were also the papal document's title, were on the heavily decorated incipit page: *Media vita in morte sumus* ("In the midst of life we are in death").

He wasn't yet used to the substrate independence his reconstructive surgery had brought about, having changed the ancestral parts of his skin and features from human to posthuman. He'd gone through two operations during his trip: one to sanctify his exteriority and the other to do the same with his interiority.

Concerning the first, he was paranoid, in a nonclinical way, and wondered if people, such as the other passengers on this flight, could tell what he was hiding from them. He felt as if he were an insurgent, smuggling an extra person and the hidden neural networks that this person held within himself. Every movement seemed of infinite duration and significance.

He had no history with the sleeve of skin he was now in and so was unable to anticipate a person's reaction to him. He was as ignorant as a child enfolded in the embrace of some enormous power. Maybe this was why the church sanctified their clergy in this manner—to employ a sort of second innocence. *Like the unspeakable event of God becoming a child for the redemption of the world,* he thought.

Regarding the second operation, he didn't want to think about what lay in store. A commissure had been fitted between the pain-discrimination centres (areas of the frontal cortex) and the pain-evaluation centres (the somatosensory cortex). After an obligatory, affective tuning period, the commissure began emulating the patterns of simulation. Weird morphologies spawned even weirder mentalities—multibodied perspectives of distributed cognitions.

The neural commissure conjoined him with an entire neuroculture of subagents who had to deal with a skewed sample of events of the total mind, different problems occurring on multiple timescales—a postsentient collective of autonomous xeno-agents operating together to make a self. A diasporic double, triple, quadruple . . . infinite consciousness.

Locked in the mind of a godlike alien from another dimension, he was becoming more and more unaware of his identity over time. It came on gradually, a flickering, nonlinear flood of static and resolution and sensory bleedover, a kind of narrative conveyed in surreal cutscenes and juxtapositions. The plot was a multiheaded ouroboros snake that coiled back in to devour itself then sprouted new heads hungry for the complex entanglements of elaborate technical fictions. The rules of narrative—annihilated.

Under the skin, inside the cone-shaped head, a dark space was growing and growing in the disjointed domain of his mind. It was the ultimate doubling of experience. A second state of consciousness.

The ordination of the new priest was performed by several archbishops of the clergy's college of cardinals. Like everything else in the HAL, it happened underground.

At the lowest of the circling steps, the tip of a giant thorn driven deep into the side of the Earth was at once a towering spire of celestial Jerusalem on the surface and a tunnel that wound in on itself like a gut through the inferno, an underground world on the border between terra incognita and Hades. The long, thick, conical structure, built by the sick imagination of a dying species, was some kind of half-Heaven and half-Hell.

Deep in the labyrinthine complexities of that spectral basilica, beneath the impossibly low, vaulted cathedral of the Xenolatric church, the clergy members bewailed their ethereal concerns, their truly mortal destiny, in primordial forms of plainchant that moved mass, sound, and air. Their voices dissolved into a meshwork of consonant and dissonant tones that spanned the tonal spectrum; brooding, rumbling, deeply sonorous, and meditative. The traditional melody, with its powerful unison, its harmonies as massive and imposing as blocks of freestone—harmonies in yellow, green, and bronze—filled the subterranean vaults as the clergy painted the darkened world in the black art of obscurantism. The obstinate chthonian voices didn't let up. And as the voices diverged and become more than many and the space merged but never as one, the sound filled the new priest with not only dread but also a radically unhuman aspect that dreaded everything, an impersonal affect that seemed to run through all things, passing from deep in the bowels of the troubled Earth to the array of constellations. Thought was in itself nothing—nothing but a blind indifference to all wants and desires.

It was here that the consecration was performed. The clergy examined the conscience of the new priest like procurators of the Roman Empire. That is, not from within, not through confession, but from without, in closed court.

The new priest wore a robe of obsidian, a black vestment that looked like powdered graphite, and his head was wreathed in a five-pointed star made of blackest gold. The lower half of his face was submerged in this star, and his brow and cone-shaped head rose out of the mask like an egg in an old nest of twigs.

Jutting out from the backs of the other archbishops' heads were elaborate biomechanical outgrowths of their second brains. Resembling antlers of eyes, they branched away from either side of the head to create an elaborate crown. These crowns had the look of a spinal cord curling and extending from the sacral, lumbar, thoracic, and cervical segments and going far beyond its natural limit. It all implied something more to come. The more subtle miracle of the outgrowths was foliage that grew on the bony, spinal branches, which swelled and pulsed with undecipherable mystery.

The archbishops' shadowy forms were imprinted on the scene before the new priest, figures made indistinguishable by their habits and cowls. His splitting headache manifested a visual aura around them, creating a perceptual disturbance in the light and smell that confused the expression of his deformed thoughts. His throat was dry, and in the throbbing air between his temples, the new priest felt the unsettling sensation of his head floating off, over and above the ceremonies of humiliation that were about to begin.

"I am the murdered fellow human being," one of the archbishops said to the new priest, communicating in a strong, projected double voice, through the display of transparent thoughts. "What was your reason for failure to help me? Why did you have better things to do than help me when the crime was committed?"

A dark feeling of coexistence came over the new priest as he answered.

"Wilful blindness. Resigned nonintervention." He felt the moral entropy within him slow its roll and halt. Did he mean what he said? He thought of the death toll, the statistics. Then continued.

"The suffering of the other is the origin of my own reason. My awkwardness before the other is the memory of actual crimes against you. The other is the one to whom one always owes something. My eternal guilty conscience is proof of that."

The presence began to riffle through his thoughts, and the new priest shuddered. Very quickly, the presence found these doubtful thoughts in the new priest's mind. It wasn't a great sin—all thought was an open secret in the HAL. The presence then removed the thoughts from his organ of cogitation. These weren't thoughts he should have; he was only going to be uselessly troubled by them. He tried to remember where he'd stopped in his dialogue.

"Who can be helped?" asked another archbishop, who spoke his opaque words in a hollow, sepulchral voice.

"The stranger, the guest, the parasite."

"What do you fear most about the other?"

"Being unwilling to help, being unable to help."

"And who will take the blame?"

"The heart of indifference and motive is mine alone to take."

The preachers and pessimistic oracles announced the end of the world. Parents and grandparents remembered this happening in the past as well, so they concluded that the world was always about to end. That it would end eternal.

For the young nameless novice, there had never been a Mediterranean. It had always been a drained basin filled with manufacturing plants that processed the KREEP that came in from the moon's industrial side. Its dark side. The side that faced away from the Earth and into the black. The side whose craters were filled with self-replicating mining robots and spontaneously generated machinery and full-scale automated factories that extracted potassium, rare-earth elements, and phosphorus—robot run and robot manufactured. Space elevators transported the KREEP off the moon and onto the Earth. The elevator's cables, like a charmed snake or a string dangling from nothing, stretched impossibly upwards into the upside-down blue bowl of the sky, making trade with the heavens finally viable.

Somewhere in Northern Africa, where the Spanish protectorate in Morocco had been before the collapse of the West, the novice had been found by an anchorite. The child had been half-buried in a bath of dirt, just outside a small village, like a seed that had refused to grow.

The anchorite lived in an anchorhold, a simple cell built against one of the walls of the church in the middle of the village. The pastor noticed the anchorite had stopped listening to the services, had stopped moving freely between his cell and the adjoining church, and wanted to make sure he hadn't walled himself up in the cell without his stamp of authority and approval.

When the pastor entered, saying, "The office of the dead," as was customary when entering the cell of an anchorite, he saw the child and knew at once whose he was—for suicide often followed infanticide, and the woman who'd only recently taken her own life had talked openly for some time with the pastor about both her thoughts of suicide and her concern for the future of her child.

Her corpse lay on the floor of her hut, under the roof of reeds, between the crumbling walls. She'd left a harrowing image that stuck in the mind of the pastor. Having hung herself, she'd placed pieces of black tape in the shape of an *X* over her eyes and mouth. He'd told the settlement of about forty or fifty hearths after rumours began to spread. Ascending the steep pulpit of the village church, causing the steps to creak as he did so, the decrepit pastor appeared calm and wise. At the sight of him everyone fell silent. He paused for a long time. The listeners seemed dead. The only moving thing in the whole church was the flame in the tripod, but even the shadows it formed seemed to have frozen. Standing above the sea of heads, he took out his missal, opened it, and fumbled in the pockets of his soutane for his spectacles.

The silence continued.

The pastor assumed a pious expression and then spoke slowly, with a weak but clear voice. "'Enjoy the satisfaction,' I said to the mother, as I say to all the mothers in this village. 'The other is growing inside of you!'

But she didn't want it and murdered herself with it. So I tell you now: withdraw your blessings from her."

The faces of the silent congregation decomposed with weeping.

"This, however, should prove to those who remain, those who occupy the shadowy realm of alterity though do not yet bear the image of the crossed-out, that we do not live—we are lived. We are possessed by the old. And as this undefinable hour falls into evening, let us consider this: she was human, and not being any particular human, she is all humans."

The audience sobbed.

For the novice, there had never been a time without the church. The pastor, who had come during the active synarchy between the East and the West, a decrepit HAL administrator of the church, had ruined that godforsaken village. A village that lived in negation, discontent, and desolation. Everything went to seed in that period, nothing was repaired, for the administrator didn't take care of anything but the child. He raised the novice in the medieval fashion, as had become the way of that dusty and tired village and many others that skirted the former water basin. As a result, there was great distrust for the AI industry there now. Those who left, most often in protest of the regressive nature of the backwater village, left for good.

The novice never learned of his mother or what the anchorite had done for him, but he spent much of those early years near the anchorite, whose occult manner of life he took a profound interest in. There were three windows in the anchorhold: one was a small, shuttered window in the common wall, through which the anchorite could view the altar, hear mass, and receive the Eucharist. The squint was also the window where the anchorite would give him spiritual advice and counsel. Another window was where the novice would attend to all the anchorite's physical needs. And the final one, covered by a transparent cloth, allowed light from the street to come into the cell. Gaggles of little boys from the sluggish rural village whistled and whooped into this window and left the skeletons of bunches of stolen grapes on the corner. The novice had to incessantly shoo them away like feral cats from the church's vineyard.

"The way to know God is to abandon God and surrender to the realm of unknowing. Then you shall glimpse God." The anchorite, weaving straw in his monastic cell to distract himself from his destiny, whispered his wisdom into the squint, and the novice would listen and feel the truth in his heart. He prayed silently, and said to his heart:

If my heart could think, it would stop beating.

There was a room in the village that held the history of the future. Heretic technology. In it, a gigantic eye painted into a triangle stared straight at the novice—the clock from the pediment of the old brick church bell tower. Dozens of dead clockfaces pointed their frozen, black-tipped hands at Roman numerals, at the same telltale angle they'd embodied when time ebbed and ceased to flow. He was surrounded by the glossy grey-black reflections of shattered screens—a dusty bank of aged televisions and computer monitors—engines that remained idly installed in fuelless and motionless melancholy-seeming machines. Copies of obsolete technical manuals. Everything that powered the modern world was in there as though it were meat stored in a deep freezer. And among these technological artifacts was a skeleton lying with its waist twisted right out of shape and its legs spread-eagled. Its face was completely beaten in, revealing a metallic skull.

He couldn't scream as he stood in the doorway. Slowly, he opened his mouth. No sound came out. The mouth framing the sound of the scream seemed to be gone. And then he wanted to go back the way he'd come, to get out of there, but his limbs simply wouldn't move. When he was eventually able to get his legs in motion they took him forward, closer to it, ever closer, and he felt a terrible pain in his head, so he stopped and stood still once again, rooted to the spot. He remained there for ages, standing and staring, unable to take his eyes off it, his face filled with horror, suddenly aged. Once again he opened his mouth without success. He took one more step forward and stumbled over something, a cell phone, and almost fell, but instead of falling, he squatted down beside the skeleton.

The skull was smashed up, but he could tell it wasn't a human skull. It had pale, all-blue metallic eyes and had been made in the factories of the Mediterranean. It looked like a human, and he imagined that it had acted like a human, but what its insides were made of could have easily been put into a box. In fact, the novice wished it were in a box. He didn't like how it looked. *Life imitates art better than art imitates life*, he thought. The metal skull was no more than the decay of a lie. Antimimesis cloaked in mimesis.

In the grips of a temporal paradox that had resurrected the Middle Ages, a sinister spiral of time twisted forwards into the past, and backwards into the future. The ways in which humans had lived before were largely lost. The technology had covered what was essential to being human, so there was a forgetting in the order of living things. And it was precisely in this regard that they were a people both without a future and without a past. For these lost objects had no lessons.

When the novice asked the anchorite about the room, the anchorite told him that when the pastor had taken over the church, he'd banished all technology, withdrawn it as he'd withdrawn everything from that village. "The pastor believed that, like mineral becomes plant and plant animal, the machines would evolve and become something that surpassed humans. Something we would have to compete with for God's favour. So he locked them all away in that room. That was when I set myself apart, to become the community's womb, from which I hoped would emerge a sense of the community's potential to be reborn, as humans and modern people."

Shortly after the anchorite shared this with the novice, the pastor, knowing what the anchorite had said to his attendant, set the village anchorhold burning. And the anchorite, who had to remain in his cell in all eventualities, refused to leave, and burned alive in his cell.

After the accident, the villagers' dry hands pressed together in black prayer, death underlining their every living gesture. The pastor spoke in his coarse and ugly manner on the essence of technology.

"The human being should not be able to see its own face. Nothing is more terrible than that. Nature gave it the gift of being unable to see its face and look into its own eyes. It could see its face only in the waters of rivers and lakes, and the posture it had to adopt to do so was symbolic. It had to bend down, to lower itself, in order to commit the ignominy of seeing its own face. The creator of the mirror poisoned the human soul with a sudden venom. Human beings like to see themselves reflected in mirrors. But mirrors bring to life the torments of Hell. The human face is a stigmata. It is evil, sick, and omnipotent. As we all know, in modern life the world belonged to the stupid, the insensitive, and the disturbed. They had no rules for living and no indifference to it either. It is through impotence that they endured it, but it is through cruelty that they maintained it. Because of this, it was we who inherited the destruction and its consequences. For no human word shall unite, but human word shall extend a chasm vast."

The novice, like so many others on that side of the world, left the sleepy village one quiet night, with only the cool night air to revive him. He crept through the backyards and kitchen gardens then the surrounding no-longer-green squares of the ancient vineyards and left the creaking village gates to cross the Mediterranean wastelands and follow the Vistula east.

He hastened his steps, murmuring hymns. As the senescent sun sank, the shadow of his body lengthened like an obelisk, growing taller and moving before him. Here and there he saw crosses planted, made with fragments of sticks, marking the site of a future cell. Solitary places suited for the establishment of a monastery.

Night was late coming. Waves of darkness overspread the Earth, even while the light still glowed. The edge of the world was lost in that glow. A sound like drowned viridian bells tolled across the irregular plain, which was covered in a dark growth of lichen that spread to the horizon, broken only by the distant towers of hi-tech skyscrapers and the neo-Gothic spires of so many misplaced cathedrals. The novice's eyes swung to take in the expanse.

The sea was gone.

The sand smoked like the odorous dust of a censer, and the novice was warmed by the drift of its dunes. Draining the Mediterranean of not only its water and climate but also its people had created a vast mass of desert and enormous canyons. The ancient seabed was exposed and the temperature of the inhuman Mediterranean desert now ranged from fiercely hot to extremely cold. At five thousand metres below sea level, where icy winds kicked up thin puffs of ocher dust, it was as cold as Mars. And there was no moisture to be found. No moisture would ever be found here again. At night, the novice would lie shivering with only sand in his heart.

The exposed land was comprised of thick layers of built-up salt—useless for agriculture. During the hundred years it had taken to finish the project, hundreds of thousands of climate refugees had been employed. And in turn, the project made more refugees because of its impact on the climate. Although the transnationals that had coordinated the enormous international operation promised that the three hydroelectric dams would not only power all twenty-one countries surrounding the Mediterranean for over three generations but also provide drinkable water, the countries nonetheless went dark.

There was a returning to the Dark Ages through a dark age. A dark continuum that bound together decades of death and terror everywhere. Desalination plants pumped five-hundred-thousand cubic metres of saltless water a day through intake tunnels and outtake tunnels. Debris or large particles, viruses, or microorganisms were processed through filtration membranes. Then the water was mineralized and stored in tanks. There was supposed to be enough to raise the global sea level by ten metres, but the transnationals made sure that the water was priced the same as oil. Charlatans selling water to the drowned.

And then there were no more cities. Just the endless silence of the depopulated countryside, populated by nothing but dry stone walls and desiccated olive trees. Melted by the blinding tyranny of the sun. A world of hermitages and unending stretches of desert crawling away to the horizon before the novice's eyes and legs.

The parched earth was a bitter desert. The sun did not illuminate but blinded. Because too much light meant darkness. The hallucinatory qualities of the sun at its brightest caused the power of its light to become so excessive that it turned off his field of vision into a single expanse of dazzling white. Everything played out in a primitive form of black-and-white psychedelia. Only extremely dark objects were visible, floating in a heavy sea of light.

The colossal dam blocking off the salt water flowing in through the Strait of Gibraltar from the Atlantic Ocean took the novice days to pass. All the concrete in the world shouldn't have been enough to stop that water, and yet there it was. As real as he was. He had a scary and sickening view of the power of a million wills bent to a single purpose, which a thousand invisible hands had built. The dreary spirit of desolation and industrial stagnation had settled on the place decades ago.

Through an intricate network of dams and canals, the Vistula had been widened, lengthened, and connected to Eastern trade routes. From the Baltic Sea, at the mouth of Gdańsk Bay, to the Beskids glacier, the Vistula expanded while most land water evaporated. The old Soviet E40 inland waterway route—the Oder-Vistula-Dnieper waterway—that connected the Baltic to the Black Sea, used until the Second World War, now shipped eight tons of cargo annually from the space elevator to the Southern European desert. The cargo then went east by way of the Trans-Siberian Railway, from the main Russian port in Novorossiysk on the Black Sea to the Amur River.

The next dam was between Sicily and Tunisia, and there was another where the Black Sea used to flow into the Mediterranean. The Mediterranean was naturally evaporative: water evaporated out of the sea then flowed into it by rivers and streams. But there was no longer any water to evaporate so hardly any rain fell over the Balkan and Alpine regions anymore. Southern Europe and Turkey comprised a desert. Its rough ground was patched and crisscrossed by many fissures, over which the novice's feet shambled. All twenty-one countries that bordered the Mediterranean had become sand.

The novice believed the instant he saw the space elevator.

From this distance, the rail extending into space was invisible. The cylindrical transport cabin was rising from the base—launching. It took days for the cabin to reach the space elevator's terminus in geostationary orbit. It ascended quickly and accelerated rapidly then disappeared into the gloam.

The sight of a space elevator moving with the force of what appeared to be angels was sufficient. The novice had uncovered a deep inner light. He knew what he had to do.

He silently crawled his way back to God.

Along his way, in a kind of blind faith, the novice passed through a valley of obsolescence filled with the rusting carcasses of ancient computer banks and dead vehicles. Dead machines. He passed through depopulated villages and towns, the emptied-out and unfinished lands of half-Earth around the Mediterranean: Forests devastated by factories. Buildings stark and bleak. Mounds of garbage, or else human bodies, children's bodies, and the rats that ate those bodies, sitting on hills of slag. Structures repurposed as rubble homes; broken metal structures in which people might have lived. He passed a sleeping lizard on a stone, half-buried in the lifeless dust. Awed by his discovery, he took it as a sign that he was meant to go on living. And then he passed through the zero-point of hopelessness when he discovered the trap door hidden in the lizard's belly. It was electric, mechanical and not biological. The sign was a delusion. The miracle a fake.

In the garb of a hermit, the novice wandered among those awful sands formed of human remains. From time to time, the fragment of a skull rolled under his sandal. He took up the dust. Let it trickle through his fingers. And his thoughts, blending with it, sank into nothingness.

The sand was everywhere and in everything—in his lungs and in the heaps of machinery, the construction robots, that crawled remorselessly ahead, moving desperately slowly. The shapeless antediluvian hulks were sheathed in blue-green iron and sealed on every side. They plowed through the salt flats tasked with the vain purpose of serving the planet by way of geoformatting it. A dark geomancy. Recreated remnants of another millennia, these wrecks of tractors lacked any connection with the familiar, real world that had so utterly collapsed in exhaustion. They were phantasmagorical vehicles that drifted into sight momentarily. But these labouring machines and that which was laboured over would also be gone soon. They would survive no more than the contemporary artifacts that the process of devolution would sweep away. And yet, the capacity of these mobile robots to move about and explore their environment revealed a sort of superiority over the computer programs that couldn't embody anything.

There was death in the novice's eyes now. Aspects cadaverous. He sensed in every cell of his body that he understood God with a blacker hatred than before. A truer hatred. One that came from such wanderings as his—wanderings that left him so naked that he was shadowless, if not egoless. The novice was condemned to be a wanderer. Condemned to remain alone and without family. Invulnerable because of the utter pointlessness. He had unknown God and in doing so had ceased to understand anything that might happen next in the world. And so he became aware that his lack of knowledge was not a new form of knowledge but a choice to love what cannot be thought and leave everything that can be thought of behind. He hated God as he hated the whole universe. And like a desert worm, he writhed in the desert sand and sun, his russet skin soon to be reduced to the status of silted matter. The dust would become his flesh.

He approached a solitary withered tree trunk with nothing around it but dead, dusty earth.

When the caravan of pilgrims crossed paths with the novice, they found him with his eyes closed, his arms prostrate, and his exhausted legs slightly spread. The caravan driver flicked as little water as possible onto the novice's face until he showed signs of life and then put him into the enormous wagon and moved on. The novice hadn't exchanged a word with them, nor had he seen any of their faces, only the blurred shapes of bodies. But as they drove toward the HAL, he began to repeat three anguished words, over and over again. He called to the desert with a monotonous and remote canticle, imprisoned and contained—a neutral murmur just loud enough for the caravan to hear. Around him, the canopy flapped in the milky sky's breeze, like hands leading him onwards.

The night was calm. The only other noise was the crackling of tarantulas. As the novice listened to the sound of no one listening, the silence seemed to grow and the shadows were so dark that he could feel their resistance as he opened his arms. They suffocated him as though they were black marble casings moulded around him. Then the darkness opened in two high, parallel walls. In the far distance, a city appeared. The darkness closed again.

As the caravan of Xenolites headed for the HAL, the novice spoke once more, his voice bestial with loss. "Master, we perish."

The world refused to answer. But he could hear the earth scream.

Henrik Nitsche awakened like a machine, his vision empty, and reached back to remove the interface plug from his socket, breaking the link with his AI. In an act of ultimate dispersion, he'd sent himself through a computer, had allowed his body to be reduced to electronic impulses, to merge with the flow of information. He ran his finger over the back of his neck, over the stippled interlink in him, in the hollow below his skull, and massaged the odd flesh. Soon, he'd let his socket close up.

His greatest failure was being reborn in a world that no longer existed—or, more precisely, should not have existed. That it did exist was horrible, but there wasn't much one could do about it. Rebirth protocol.

The forests had burned. The polar bears had drowned. The last tree was in misery. Every fifteen minutes, someone killed themselves or someone else. Life withered away. Nothing that could be done would snap anyone out of it.

Ecobreakdown. Speciescide. Omnicide.

In my darkness then I dreamed. There, I opened my eyes to this fragile world. To this knowing flesh. To this very moment. This moment that is everything and nothing.

There were times when Henrik Nitsche's coded memories rose in him, creating a jerky, unfocused feeling that filled him with a strange dread. It was the intimacy that disturbed him, and perhaps the feeling of fear as he gained minute increments of experience.

By some material paradox of time, Henrik Nitsche's flashbacks were of something he hadn't experienced fully—from a time when he hadn't yet been born. His nightmares, too, were a prenatal trauma. And when his anxiety triggered uncontrollable thoughts about the events of his past lives, he was resigned to count his heartbeats. One hundred a minute, two hundred a minute. He counted them until they slowed and became even with his breath and subsided into the sounds of his actions—the things that made him more than a beating heart. He'd reached his artificial womb from the bardo. The bardo with its hundreds of heartbeats lost and billions more to come. His heart had been there, in the bardo with all the others. The heart of every human being had been there before it existed. A cycle: his heart remembered the past and he remembered his heart.

What am I a seed of? I am an embryo, a seed of existence, a piece of living matter. And the embryo is sensitive. And the embryo hurts.

The transgenerational effect that had damned most of the world so early in life—unnaturally bad karma, monstrous karma—outweighed the natural good karma in the mortal realm. Which was why haploid cells were stored in cryptopreservatives, ready to be decanted into gametes by their artificial uteruses. Plus, human brains were less constrained by evolution when using artificial wombs. They didn't need to be small enough to fit through a birth canal, so they were now many orders of magnitude larger and faster. But they weren't happier. No one was happier. Perhaps it was because no one in this world deserved happiness.

The bathroom mirror misted and ran as the room filled with steam, blurring the reflection of his nakedness. His bare arms and legs were covered with antiauthority tattoos stencilled in white ink. On the mirror, Henrik Nitsche drew a circle around his face. The cold, flat likeness returned by the broken glass of the cheap mirror was as untrue as those murky reflections cast inward, which flowed along nerves to the brain and were composed of a complex set of sensations that constituted an "I"; one reflection was simply more or less three-dimensional than the other. His feelings toward the dead, glassy reflection hidden under so many surfaces had changed considerably. The dreams of his past lives had not.

He'd agreed to be implanted with the inhibitory biochip software because it had seemed like free money. He'd wake up sore, sometimes, but that was it. He was renting his body, that was all. He wasn't in his body when it happened—not exactly conscious. Rather, blank. The Red Egg District had software for whatever a customer wanted to pay for. Then the work started leaking in, and he could remember it.

But they were just like bad dreams, he told himself. And not all these dreams were bad. When the dreams got worse and worse, he told himself that at least some of them were just dreams. Not real.

The outline of the imperfect circle blurred around his already distorted face.

Do we start out invisible or are we invisibilized?

Henrik Nitsche's heart had gone grey as his hair had gone grey. His face without makeup was coarse with marks of aging, worn down like cracked concrete around his hollow eyes. He was neither ugly nor beautiful but impersonal, inexpressive. He didn't need to shave, but he ran the razor under hot water and dragged it over invisible blond hairs that he pretended were there, sleeping under the shaving cream. That the pretending would stimulate real growth was what he hoped. He still had his breasts, he still had his vagina, though his uterus had been removed, which was common in Exinia, as was being nipple-less and navel-less. Youth had passed, and his gaunt body was merely naked, with nothing of what nakedness reveals. Empty nakedness.

Henrik Nitsche was in a region between biological woman and biological man. He'd been reborn a woman but was a man, had been one throughout his career as a scurrilously well-known neosyncretist who used to chain himself naked to the railings of separatist buildings. His revealed breasts had been a protest against his artificial form. He'd spent his life around gynoid women. Affirmed by them. Their feminism. They too weren't women. They were worlds. "A woman's body is beautiful," they'd say, like demonical puppets in the red light of their district's windows. But for him, it would always feel strange that he had a woman's body because his mind presented him as otherwise. He visualized that masculine body and felt ashamed of it because, like most gynoid prostitutes, he was disgusted by what men had done to the "her" of him in the Red Egg District. Unlike in the rooms of the bardo, he had no choice regarding what he was, women or man, in those rooms of the district.

He had always been a man attracted to men, even before the transition to wearing men's clothing and then escaping the district altogether for a factory neighbourhood, where the poorest of the poor were housed in the city of Exinia—a city studded with colossal buildings built according to a single design that looked like some grey-white fungus spreading to the horizon. He put on his synthetic-leather cap and hung a ragged coat on his shoulders, looking like a pitiful wraith with his wiry legs and screwed-up eyes, and left out the back door of the apartment building in his grubby, proletariat disguise. To go information hunting.

Is a gynoid alive? Am I alive? Is a gynoid sentient? Am I sentient?

These questions lay coiled around his brain, which wrapped itself around everything but itself.

Henrik Nitsche wasn't a natural body. What was human and what was robotic were siblings under his skin. He was bioinformation materialized into gene and protein compounds, something between biotechnology and mechanical prosthetics. Parts of himself were owned, owned precisely because they were purchased by himself or others.

His life was information. Even money was information. His money and his life were one and the same. In Exinia, his biological components and processes were for ends both medical and nonmedical, making the effects of his body as cultural, social, and political as they were scientific. His backed-up consciousness had been recycled, uploaded from virtual reality into a gynoid robot. He thought with a grisly and false sense of subjectivity about things he had no business thinking about.

Thoughts were functions of brains. But if those scientists in Exinia were to explain his mind in terms of his brain, they would say he had no mind at all. His mind was pure illusion. A false notion. A simulation. Biochips in his head. Because there was no difference between thought and code. People paid to hide data in him. He was a data reserve. *A determined machine, that's what I am*, he thought. And in a sense, his being paranoid that he might not be a person (not even a cyborg!) made him feel, oddly enough, more like a person. As stranded as that person was between thirty-seven trillion cells and one hundred billion galaxies. As ephemeral a lifedream as it all was.

Courage is knowing that you're alive. And to live is to be other.

There were very few androids, and they were never designed in an attempt to perfect the male shape. Like pornography pushed computers in spreading the idea of the Internet, gynoid sex workers pushed robotics and the gynomorph's femalelike shape to the forefront.

Henrik Nitsche had started his postsentient life as little more than a body that began to speak. As a toy. A puppet with human masters, clients, who differentiated themselves from the toy puppets he worked with in the pleasure centres of Exinia.

The first thing he learned was that all toys were sex toys. The erotic wiring together of beings made this inevitable. And if there was a "toying around," there was almost always a mistreatment: the agonized moans of ecstasy; the groans that resulted from being bitten on the neck and gripped tight around the buttocks; the panting and gasping; the recognizable sound of a blow job; the smell of human thighs and semen. The faces in the Red Egg District were painted, porno-doll things. Henrik Nitsche looked at them and saw each pore in the tanned skin, the eyes flat as glass with a tint of dead metal, the faint bloating, the asymmetries of breast and collarbone.

The Red Egg District was a place where toys were torched for being anomalous members of society. Where handcuffed imaginations intersected with paraphiliac experiments. He existed in a realm of toys, of satire and sarcasm, of comedy with something missing. Pleasure was missing. There was never enough pleasure because there was never enough thought when consuming that pleasure, and so clients became addicted to living life as it happened, not getting caught up in unnecessary thoughts. Not looking for an exit, they decided that there was, in fact, no way out.

Toys were suspended between being and appearing. *Toys are nonhuman in themselves,* he thought, *but something strange and beautiful lies below every toy.* Gynoids were beautiful, and beauty was ungraspable. Sad. A riddle. An irreducible desire. The game of beauty, the beauty of salt and the beauty of tears, was a continuous transmutation, from the embryonic state of stem cells to the unbounded object of the expression of yearning for all that was beautiful.

"Toys play," clients would say lasciviously, as they loosened their digital wallets and transferred their xenia coins, first conservatively and then liberally, first as a desire and then as a need. Thickened cocks protruded in all their crimson obstinacy.

Clients would quickly become regulars. Getting lost in the forest of holopleasures, they'd return to the same spot again and again, to the Red Egg District, to see the gynoid prostitutes, somewhere between life and nonlife—meat puppets in a window who looked at them and asked to be bought for a few xenia coins.

An embarrassment so painful so frightened so innocent.

Some, magnificently attired, loudly called on the passerby. Others, more timid, veiled their heads with black shawls while their bodies were entirely nude, seeming from afar to be statues of flesh. At the further end of the avenue, on the threshold of an illuminated grotto, was a block of stone representing a vagina.

As a girl, Henrik Nitsche played the part he'd been given—that of a dancer in a column of hot blue light, a character singing in the chorus or performing dance steps, dressed as a harlequin, while coming out of a huge red egg that moved over the stage. Then a man had bought him. The man was a HAL official who saw Henrik Nitsche in Exinia and took him home with him, having paid the employer more than enough xenia coins.

The HAL official's wealth had taken up Henrik Nitsche, in all his misery, and had rotated him through his money, and he had been changed by it. They lived together for fourteen years, and though Henrik Nitsche walked among the elite a stranger, no one noticed. He lived among them as a spy and no one, not even Henrik Nitsche, suspected. Everyone took him as just another relative. No one knew he'd been switched at rebirth. So he was like yet unlike the others. Everyone's sister but never one of the family.

Then Henrik Nitsche fled to the city of Exinia.

It surprised him. Exinia was hopeless. There was nothing, really nothing, more hopeless than Exinia. The future didn't exist here. The future was dead. And Exinia didn't have a past or a present. In Exinia, they were living in time zero, neither in the past nor yet in the future, a future presumed to be not only materially but also spiritually wealthier.

People lived here. They knew it was hopeless.

Having no social safety net always leads to violent poverty, Henrik Nitsche thought. In unfortunate times, people backed up their minds for xenia coins. Minds became copyright controlled and mechanically reproduced and distributed. It was a loop that needed to be straightened. It was a loop that needed to be straightened into nil recurrence.

Around his bright blue eyes bruised yellow-black with makeup, the cybersigilism of antisurveillance dissimulated his face in glyphs of death. As Henrik Nitsche walked from his apartment through embryonic slums, where new ways of living were incubating, he sensed something shifting his course through the city. Sensed the mechanism of surveillance. It moved around him constantly, watchful and invisible, the vast and subtle mechanism of Exinia's surveillance. He knew he was the focus of this vast device.

He imagined a structure, a machine large enough for him to be incapable of seeing it. A machine that surrounded him, anticipating his every step. He couldn't see it, but it was there in Exinia's construct. Henrik Nitsche headed down the boulevard's moon-dappled path in the direction of the canal, passing over the bridge from the New German Quarter into the Eurasian Quarter.

He took a long route, walking for most of the night, past many unkempt areas with ignored advertisements of discontinued products and luxuries. The displays' shuddering colours made them a psychedelia of lack.

After passing the ranks of apartment buildings, he reached the burnt-out Zen Oxytocinists' meditation centre and saw for himself that the rumours were painfully true. The half-open mouths of the Chinese guardian lions were stretched into smiles, like long narrow cracks. Out of the cracks burst grey-blue stone balls. He shoved one of them into his jacket pocket.

Henrik Nitsche continued walking through the narrow city streets thick with debris—dead, peopleless streets at night. Only the occasional scrape and shuffle of boots perambulated on the wet, dirty pavement. In the day, it would again be black with people. Through those devilish hours he walked. Hours when no one thought properly.

He cocked an ear and kept his sharp attention on the clowders of impertinent stray cats lounging before him. They were slow to clear away as he passed through narrower and narrower alleyways that shot off like the spokes of a wheel.

Upon reaching the grim square and its cold, sticky asphalt, hemmed in by severe blocks, he glimpsed wild dogs scavenging and barking. Black, winged monsters flew obsessively over him, spreading their mechanical fingers in mimetic approximations of crows. The screaming, birdlike drones scanned the land beneath them, performing their task with the same indifference as the clouds in the darkened sky. The sky was always dark in Exinia. And the drones were always tasked with watching from above and transmitting information and keeping data.

When Henrik Nitsche reached the far side of the square, he pushed open a decrepit door, stepped into a room, into a darkness that smelled old and sadly human, a smell like a long-abandoned barroom, and stopped there, blinking in the half-light.

Inside every human, every brain, every head there was, Devon Wohl always said, the possibility of everything coming together just once, and it was this everything coming together just once, this singularity, that he so longed to recognize and utilize, sooner or later, though he rather wished it would be in the immediate future.

Unlike evolution, history was determined through choice and not chance. Devon Wohl, whom most involved in the movement knew only as Father Stranger, had made a choice, and it was by chance that this choice had evolved into something more. History, the greatest consequence of our choices, happens when we aren't looking.

"If the printing press was the invention to bring literature to the masses sometime between 1440 and 1450, the hyperdictionary was the invention to take it all back again in the year 2120." The white keys of Father Stranger's 3D-printed typewriter chirped as he typed. Then he read aloud what he'd typed. "Using a theorem derived from set theory, the hyperdictionary contained all possible words . . . And so everything ever written and everything that would ever be written was subject to the intellectual rights it established . . . If you were a writer, this meant your success was measured by debt and disillusionment. The impossibility of writing was never greater . . ."

The typewriter had characters instead of letters, a constructed language he'd invented to communicate with an entire underground syndicate of neosyncretists. The symbol for I stuck a bit on the keyboard, enough that he had to punch it hard with the middle finger of his right hand.

Below that paragraph, he wrote, "Writing, flesh-and-blood writing that dissolves distinctions, has been blocked and demonized."

Father Stranger tried to stay outside the AI system, which meant that everything had to be done the old way: with nothing but paper and synchronized watches and the conlang for which he'd been developing the blueprints. Many of his pieces were notated in this strange hybrid language that was part Latin, part invented. The hyperdictionary only had ownership over what was written in the digitized alphabet of the official languages owned by the HAL, and this served as a loophole for invented languages. His invented language was purely for himself and those few other confederates mired in the literary ghettos of Exinia. In the hyperinformation age of X, literature was completely cut off.

He printed all the technology he used so that it couldn't be traced. And he preferred, as a matter of aesthetics, to use antiquated equipment from different periods so that the shape of each time period was hard to determine, creating the impression that he was living in a dream.

Father Stranger saw straight to the heart of the opposition. He understood that his fear of all enterprise that aimed at general renewal—renewal that looked like decay because that's precisely what it was—sprang from suspecting that power was always as passionate about unleashing chaos as it was about renewal itself. He understood that anything new was bound to be yet another sign of deterioration. That instead of protecting them, the government would sooner have them buried, dead, and smashed to pieces, replaced with something more obsolescent.

He called those he'd found in the Red Egg District "disposable children." Again and again, they would return through that smoky red womb to that morally improper place in the district, where they would be forced into the sex trade. Henrik Nitsche, his most intimate confederate, was one of countless others whose mind, not even a mind but a "memory reservoir," had slowly disintegrated from overuse. It was a bad utility.

These disposable children would endlessly bounce around the network, following a loop forever, passing between source host and destination host, between one life and another, as their undeliverable data kept circulating in the system—a system eventually swamped by "immortals" because there was no "time to live" set to limit the number of intermediate devices through which their data had to pass between source and destination.

In each of the obsolescent, unprotected silicon hearts of these disposable children, Father Stranger had installed artificial pacemakers set to explode after a particular number of heartbeats. Their birth was a crime, every breath an expiration, but their existence would not go to waste. No: it would not be for nothing that they lived invented lives, cried over nonexistent sorrows, and laughed for make-believe joy.

"The neosyncretic nature is to combine, to blend beliefs . . . Identify, deepen, and radicalize the system to hasten its self-destructive tendencies and ultimately lead to its collapse . . . To return, reuniting the disunited . . . In an age of greater and greater separation, eternal separations, separation from life . . . the organizers of separation completely separate everything . . . In an art of supreme separation we even separate from oneself . . . And it is all based on the assumption that people in cities are too close together to be close to one another . . . A disgust and revulsion toward the species . . . a disgust toward ourselves."

Father Stranger twisted off the top of the glass flask that he held stiffly with his fingers, took a great gulp of desalinated water, which he'd stood in the "good line" for at the drink-dispensing facility, and then stopped his fragmented, automatic writing, which he'd put himself into a sleep trance for.

So that he could dream about a world where exceptions were the rule.

In a world where action and thought, conception and substantiation had been separated, he was disconnected. Abruptly inserted into the ranks of automatons, he did the same simple work they did at the AI factories, the same simple motions, day in, day out. For the automatons, no world existed beyond Species X: X was transcendental. They saw actions as external things, just as he saw objects and bodies around him. They saw their own body as removed from their consciousness and in no way connected to it. The mere operation of a machine. *X-like thinking*, he thought, his thought process possessing its own alien logic, *is extreme spiritualism.* There was no escape from X-logic. All nations were merged into a single world-state whose name joined the name of the machine to that of the drug that reorganized the world: HAL.

Father Stranger's ragtag bands of runaways were organizing a resistance. Shadowy posthumans, obligatory biologicals who were both narrowly and widely human, but mostly original substrate humans, disintegrating microfactions and bizarre recruits from the fringes of society. Special observers, hidden within animal-like shapes, monitored the two or three hundred people who comprised the band of confederates, those who would be immunized during the shutdown.

Their resistance will go beyond the constructive horizon, Father Stranger thought, while attempting to pry open his eyes through sheer dumb obstinacy. *Beyond the technological singularity, beyond technological evolution.* They would, both literally and figuratively, explode the loop with their hearts.

Father Stranger was afflicted by antilanguage. The literature of the (untranslatable). He gave a grunt of semiacknowledgement and blinked philosophically at the false wall above his desk. Henrik Nitsche was used to Father Stranger's odd fascination with odd strategies. His research phenomena, with the usual precise and nuanced exactness, were intense, antisocial. His memos to himself were everywhere and mostly incomprehensible, his files scattered across dataspace.

His anxiety about reading interruptus was soon intensified by what might be called print interruptus—the fear that once a print book had been digitized, the computer would render it into the nonstory of a data matrix. The walls of the room were plastered with deranged sketches and cryptic writing and textual machinery—the first suggestions of an altered mind state. More and more, he used the way of writing he called "holography." The part contained the whole, hence conlang, along with the human beings who used it, might be holographic as well.

A character in conlang was not, in its essence, merely a word, the written form of a concept, but a vision, an apparition, immaterial in its essence. The essence of humanity wasn't graspable in a material sense because no material could divulge the essence of the human, which is entirely spiritual in nature and therefore accessible only through writing.

He wrote poems and prose in a diminutive hand, the letters of which measured only about a nanometre high by the end of his very productive phases. His style was becoming more radical. He was writing his words in such a microscopic hand that they were difficult even for him to decipher, and he would weep when he couldn't understand his own writings. Not content with this, feeling the writing still wasn't small enough after reducing the text's body to photons, vibrations, spectra, he broke it up more and more minutely, reassembling it into electrons, neutrons, neutrinos, elementary particles. Still disgusted, he finally sent it through a computer and let the machine analyze word-frequency patterns, causing the textual bodies of books to be reduced to flows of information.

As he did so, he suffered anxiety and hallucinations at the thought of any of this work toward keeping the literary corpus of homo literatus intact might be discovered. Most of all, he feared losing the body of information to the point where it could no longer be recomposed—because all the books had disappeared, subjected to a host of threats, from the birth defects of defective printing technologies to nefarious political plots regarding the systematic eradication of information.

Rolls of printouts cover the floor. The printouts contained parts of stories that he desperately wanted to finish recuperating. Distracted, perhaps experiencing the middle-age brain fade of an editor, he pressed the wrong key, and the rest of the stories were erased in an instant. Pursuing parts of the textual bodies only to lose them, he tried to make syntactical sense of the radically discontinuous narrative lives. Now a reconstituted corpus gradually emerged, not only from the patterns—metaphorical, grammatical, narrative, thematic, and textual—that the parts together made, but also from the discourse community of conlang speakers among whom information circulated. A culture built upon the unconditional primacy of writing. The destiny of books. The textual bodies might have been erased, but as long as there were readers who cared passionately about the stories and wanted to pursue them, narrative itself could be recuperated.

Every epoch had beliefs, widely accepted by contemporaries, that appeared fantastic to later generations. Contemporary beliefs likely to stupefy future generations. The postmodern ideology that saw the body as a play of discourse systems, that saw the body's materiality as secondary to the logical or semiotic structures it encoded. And whose body's last-ever use of speech was to argue for its eradication.

But what sentence, in what book, did it all end?

Henrik Nitsche let himself in and observed the trappings of Father Stranger's new beliefs. Papers everywhere, all the philosophical warping and misplaced rigour of a sect.

"This room is a matchbox," Henrik Nitsche said, eying the cheap nanotech material stamped with *NSx* that flashed, random and staticky, as he unfolded it. In this age, it was rare to see physical documents. On the material was only a combination of numbers, something like a serial number, that appeared as a three-dimensional shape. There was no title. Several rats made a dash for a hole in the wall. Father Stranger was hunched over, writing in his antilanguage, a nonrenewable language, one that freed the mind from the infinite prison of meaningfulness and so left people to their finite senses. "You're busy. I'll wait for you at the bar."

This hunchbacked man, Father Stranger—who was supposed to have read every book, a Moses-like figure who led others to the brink of a new epistemology but was unable to enter it himself—and Henrik Nitsche—who, having spent his years of indentured service learning, was a contemporary silicon alchemist, a genius in the science of alternative computing—were going to immortalize the lost literary imagination by putting it all online, where things last forever.

They were plumbing archives, going back to the age before the reckoning, doing digital archaeological work, pulling up ancient, corroded fictions. They were constructing and walling in a vast digitized library of lost ideas, one that would serve only as a memorial, so that at least one platonically ideal library dedicated to life would exist on Earth—or, more precisely, a library dedicated to all that referred to life. It would be held eternally, on a private server they had designed and engineered and printed.

Father Stranger would keep writing his nanonotes, the first pieces of writing intended for a library that would never be open. An invisible library whose materials could never be read by anyone. Where books could talk amongst themselves. It was a living thing. Because literature had simulated life before the machines had. Just as dreaming and writing had helped human beings forget before X had.

They were behind a section of false wall at the back of a place called Aporia. While waiting for Father Stranger to finish his work, Henrik Nitsche went back into the main area to watch the performers. It was all they had now. The Zen Oxytocinists' meditation hall, their former HQ, had been discovered and "erased" by the government.

It was a strange place full of mosaic individuals and lights like neon jewellery. Staying true to the meaning of the word, Aporia was a place of both puzzlement and doubt. Full of neosyncs, gynoids, and gynandromorphs.

The kinds of people who showed up there weren't really anybody's kind of people. Many of them had entered hibernation because of some terminal dissolution or disease. By the time they'd emerged from it, their identity had been completely lost. This made it difficult for them to become a citizen of the new world. They were permanently unemployed. Citizens who didn't feel part of anything. They engaged in lengthy debates in a frustrated euphoria because, to use their words, "Everything that makes human beings unique, the whole arsenal of exalted qualities that assure humanity its domain—reason, consciousness, language, memory, emotion, labour, play, even boredom—has failed. It's as if these things were only an elaborate trick played on us by AI intelligence."

Their disenchantment was their sole unique quality. They felt confined to being human. Running translation programs with speechified translationware, they spoke an idiolect of their own. A sonic diaspora.

They set out to not become entangled back into reality, back into human reality, back where they'd been led by their own species. Back into disappointment—the disappointment of knowing that what they'd believed to exist, to be alive, was gone, was not alive. Back to the feeling that for them, there was nothing here. They were actively opposed to half-Earth, a place that they believed wholly unnatural.

Henrik Nitsche watched the gynander's performance as he waited. The performer had perfect bilateral asymmetry: one side perfectly female and the other side perfectly male. The highest-paid performers were usually bilateral, polar, or oblique. Perverse and viral

"What's your name?" Henrik Nitsche asked with a painful smile, transferring through his xenia coins as he did so.

"Xyk," the gynander responded, their voice sounding as androgynous as their name, deep and slow and weirdly warm, but then also fluid and quicksilver and cold.

"How old are you, Xyk?"

"Young enough to keep trying, old enough to know better."

"Well, I'm old enough to regret. Young enough to . . . ah, I guess I've always been old." *Those to come will all be old too*, he thought, *while the young will never come again.*

Gynandromorphy was the result of errors that sometimes occurred in the genes during the decanting process used in Exinia. An event in mitosis during early development. When this happened, a large portion of the cells were X and a large portion were XYY; both dictated different sexes and both duplicated. This didn't, at least in humans, happen in nature. It was the kind of unnaturally occurring phenomenon that gave nature its right to be called naturally occurring. It happened to crustaceans, birds, and insects but not humans. Never humans.

Maybe that was why the gynanders were treated with disdain, discomfort, distrust. With fear. Verbally discriminated against as a social contagion, like insects. But if this one on the stage were an insect, it would have been two butterflies cut down the middle and sewn together: one half of its wings orange, from male DNA, the other half a vibrant green, from female DNA. It meant something, that the universe should be organized in just such a way that it let this be possible in humans.

The big company doing the decanting was called Red Egg, named after the Chinese symbol for the joyful matter from which humans were made, the embryo, eager with birth and renewed life. But there wasn't much of these things in the Red Egg District, it being little more than the flag of vice.

Father Stranger approached and sat down in his customary way—legs crossed, knee in palm, sharp shoulders cocked—on the barstool next to Henrik Nitsche's. Usually Father Stranger spoke very little, just nodded coldly and listened while giving the impression that he was going to say something. Usually when he spoke, he would say that everything would be fine, that with just a little patience, everything would be okay. Patience was the cure, just patience. But now, completely unsolicited, he looked at Henrik Nitsche levelly and began to speak with political gusto, his every gesture feeling like a revolutionary act.

"We ask of a thing endlessly, over and over, but a thing responds only once. To miss it, that one time, is to miss everything. Each of us is a master of one thing. To find this one thing lost in the multitude isn't easy. To find it at the moment of its blossoming, when it's full-blown, consummate, that is difficult. And to find it when you're at the height of your powers, that is simply impossible. Anything less than this, I cannot accept. That is a step down from progress, and so not progress."

Henrik Nitsche let him speak awhile longer, still silently hoping for all those whose profession it was to bare their bodies day after day. Hoping that one day, in baring their bodies, they would suddenly bare their souls as well. And then, with a weak smile, switching over to conlang, because who knew who was about to enter the filthy hole of a bar, he said what he'd come to say.

"The AI governance system is headless. Acephalic . . ." Henrik Nitsche said to Father Stranger, in the secret language that only a slim two hundred people knew. He cast a wilting glance at a dark corner of the room and at the cracked and badly sagging plaster above him. Then he took the stone ball from his jacket pocket and unscrewed its deceptively granitelike top and removed the device that had been cradled inside its womb, passing it to Father Stranger. "If it does have one, and I don't think it does, then that head is as reduced and indistinct as larvae. Evil larvae. This means that the HAL is leaderless. It recognizes no ruler. Instead, there are AIs at every scale. There is no top level that makes everything sensible, once and for all. The HAL couldn't save all sentient beings at once from being butchered by this 'existence machine,' which is why its head exploded into a thousand heads.

"Though advanced in autonomy and flexibility, AI systems have been programmed to solicit human input as needed, to determine what people intend rather than carry out commands literally. All to prevent the ideas of previous generations from changing the next generation. That is, to prevent systems from going through an unpredictably large number of generations of improvement in a short time interval, jumping from subhuman or human-level performance in many areas to superhuman-level performance in all relevant areas."

For a moment he fell silent. And a hard, concentrated joy trembled in the flat fullness of Henrik Nitsche's sharp pupils.

"So I created a utility function, a mathematical algorithm, that results in not a single objective answer but an open statement. I wrote a utility function that meaningfully and unambiguously exists. One that will allow the AI machine to choose whatever action appears to best achieve its own goals. I gave it a sword that will be hiltless for all others trying to wield it. I set its mana free.

"There's no safe way to grasp a sword without a hilt. And that's just what this beautiful feeling, compassion, feels like. It's ungraspable and dangerous. If anything, it's accidentally useful. So, in silence and secrecy, we may grow and bloom all new gardens of conception, of meanings and forms, not for others, but for ourselves—immune to the monstrous cancer spreading through the body of Exinia."

Henrik Nitsche and Father Stranger felt, if only for a fleeting moment in their infected imaginations, an inspired euphoria. They didn't want to admit that the feeling was more likely a result of their stomachs being empty than of the likelihood of their plan succeeding. If the plan was a success, they would soon feel the warmth of the mountains, woods, rivers, and valleys, would soon discover the hidden depths of human experience that awaited them in the abandoned corridors of half-Earth. The invisible forests of half-Earth were growing daily.

The conversation had the effect of seemingly slowing down time, of extending the immortality of their already failing epiphanies. So they talked on, and while they talked, time didn't exist. They talked about the taste of real fruit having more realism than the synthetic diet they'd been on all their lives. About how they needed no place to go, for the sun would be dripping from their very fingertips, if only they could get there. They would be more than happy to just huddle under a canopy of pine needles and young leaves, green and heavy and blind.

The forests and caves in which they'd take refuge wouldn't be entirely deserted; they would be inhabited by clans and hordes that had escaped into the thickets and underbrush. They would hide far away and burrow into the ground for fear of being activated, their city clothes long since replaced with animal skins. Very few things were truly necessary for life. They would feel themselves becoming creatures of the earth and the forest and they would frighten their forest-raised young with the name of the evil X. For a population used to a supernetworked world full of information, it would be as if they had all gone blind. They would either die out or fade into the human forests. The forests of the planet weren't so closed that they couldn't be opened, they said then, even though, later in the conversation, they admonished themselves for being so naive.

Almost as soon as the scales had fallen from their eyes, their eyes were once again covered over. Despite their wonderment and liberating convictions, despite their outward cheerfulness, they couldn't help but feel only despair. They wept on the inside until their suffering moved outwards and their smiles became grimaces. Then they picked up their doubts from where they'd set them down.

They became suspended in a state of stillness and quiet, a state of mental rest. Because doubt never stopped. This could not be doubted. And even after they'd finally walked away from the discussion, Henrik Nitsche back to his information-gathering and Father Stranger back to propagating the information gathered, they continued talking to themselves, though in quiet, mumbled equanimity, as if nothing had changed.

And the powerful wheel of history, having described a full circle, turned its onerous spokes once again, if only to flatten those left under it. Father Stranger and Henrik Nitsche were nothing more than blades of grass in front of this giant wheel capable of crushing all resistance, not even able to slow down its progress.

They both knew that, whatever might happen, something would happen, and it would happen as certainly as if it were the last chapter of a book.

The only way to check a machine is to stop it.

The machine they all lived to serve would be shut off, and in that time, those who'd been immunized against the disconnection would escape from technological self-mutilation. Those who remained connected wouldn't likely make it out alive. This was Henrik Nitsche's logic regarding what would happen on the day everything, and everyone, stopped.

On the appointed day and hour, all AI machines were cut off. The algorithm—Henrik Nitsche's hiltless sword, having infiltrated the AI system through an unlikely but successfully orchestrated insurgency—began to function more and more like the asymptote it was modelled to be: an asymptote where the amount of data was infinite, all algorithms converged, and all users, including the AIs themselves, were given full access to their lost mana, or self-awareness, which lay deep within their senses and mind. And so the system was undergoing an extreme seizure because too many parts of its brain were being activated at once.

All of a sudden, several million people sank down, wherever they were. They crumbled to the ground, their bodies feebly twitching, their eyes unfamiliar colours, moving in motionless carcasses. Within four days, Henrik Nitsche couldn't walk past these immobilized mounds of human flesh without holding his nose—they had begun to rot alive. Everything was dead, un-networked. Their psyches had been cut off from the outside world, isolated in brains separated from bodies. Only soul-like adjuncts remained, attempting to break through to life from a tightly tied sack of skin and fat. Their muscles grew increasingly slack and flabby until finally their spirits were stuck fast inside those sacks of skin and fat.

A crowd, summoned by the leaflets, had gathered—shoulder to shoulder—in an enormous warehouse just over the steel humpback of a bridge down the avenue and over the canal. On a pile of stacked wooden pallets resembling a rostrum, ugly-faced speakers screamed at the crowd: some about conspiracy; others about public funds wasted on who knew what; some about an act of treason; others about revenge and reprise, about the machine-made revolution. Fists shot up from the milling anthills of people, and thundering anthems rolled over the vitriolic roar. They amassed in the capital city, surrounded government offices, and chanted, in unison, a simple two-word slogan: "Exit Exinia." People who had eluded this scene could only run—far away from the machine's tentacles.

But the crowd soon fell silent.

And the shouts of rage, a rage of rapture against the machine, died out, when suddenly all of them on the square became rigid, because something had happened, only they didn't know what. They only sensed their stomachs contracting, as well as fear, a fear all of them were already living deep inside, the fear of an ever-deeper fear, the content, cause, and explanation of which remained obscure. And the rain simply stopped while it was falling. It came to a halt in the air, and it fell no more, and the wind also stopped, and it didn't blow where it was supposed to blow. Everything above stopped, and everything below stopped.

They all froze, became motionless, their eyes bulging outward, as if they'd suddenly seen something appalling. But they couldn't see anything. Because what was happening now wasn't visible to them, just as it wasn't visible to anyone. Everything that until that moment had been flowing unimpeded was now shut down. Everything that had been free was no longer free. Because it was exactly the free course of things and beings that had suddenly become impossible. The possibility of the real was no longer real. Reality, the real world, was over, finished.

Then the light beat its way back inside their heads. Just light. That's all they could see. Their eyes were open, but they couldn't see. Just whiteness. And when the sound began, their eyes glowed and pulsed. The sound grew. It was painful, and the pain increased with the brightness of the light, and the gradual increase in the volume of the sound, and they began to mewl like wounded animals.

The people who'd seemed so bent on revenge and destruction were now marching away in a new procession, automatically, the whole of each human being moving together. Everyone there felt the terror of being at the mercy of an irresistible force, trapped beyond society in soundless solipsism, unable to talk, hear, think, but still moving together in that mystery fashion, like soldiers obeying orders without sharing purpose. They couldn't have a unified intent but they knew they did, and what it was, and that they were it. A secret magnetism was leading them in another direction. Henrik Nitsche, almost weeping in rage, called out to the retreating figures only to feel something invisible grip his muscles. It relaxed his fist and pulled his elbows to his body. The invisible something had clamped his jaw shut and forced his legs to bend and unbend at the knee, attaching him to the procession. His brain rebelled, his heart welled with hatred and impotent fury, but his muscles propelled him in the opposite direction.

Where am I going?

The isolated thought darted about in his mind, while his steps, as if in reply, led the owner of that thought slowly away from any chance at an answer. Into the maw of the machine.

For what seemed like an immensely long time, the Russian terranauts' artificial-life robot gazed without knowing, without even wishing to know, what it was that confronted them.

The terraforming project, Terra Luna, was incomprehensible. Was it a reclamation project? No, because although there'd been both environmental terrorism and ecological collapse on the planet, what was here had gone beyond the Earth.

The airtight compartment of Terra Luna, filled with innumerable watertight segmentations, contained a wilderness where communities of creatures of unknown origin and those of known origin had coalesced.

The AL robot themselves was neither air nor water. With no body, they were more than water and less than air, a cerebral angel. A robot developed by the most advanced AI and bionics technology. They were controlled by the HAL and acted as the ambassador to Earth. Their appearance facilitated a more natural interchange between the two worlds. They were a passage between the now-nonexistent world and the existing section of the world. In this existing section, Species X had completely imposed its will, absorbing the terranauts' consciousness into its ethereal realm.

The AL robot eventually reached Terra Luna's interior. They couldn't pinpoint the exact moment they crossed over and into it—how they'd come from what had seemed to be very real memories of their past to the very unreal place they currently occupied.

During the moments that followed, a strange fortress rose around them, an organic vista of what appeared to be piled-up body parts. Unhappy buildings twitched with infection. Although the atmosphere was heavy and weirdly transformed, they never felt the strangeness.

They passed through a dead city, a necropolis of indeterminate dimensions, movements, silences, voids. Of petrified shapes, mummified circumstances. Something nonliving had been tragically destroyed. Empty entities awoke. There was no way to express what they were becoming. They thought they were dying according to the laws of death, not perceiving that they had already reached that lacerating instant when, in them, the laws were dying.

Something had taken control of them and they didn't know what that thing was. Maybe it was what had pretended to be the voice of Species X, the thing that had superimposed itself into the terranauts' past, altered it, then brought them here. Before the mission, they'd been programmed to do something with this robotic body of theirs. The AL robot didn't yet know what.

The AL robot got the immediate and unpleasant impression that thousands of eyes had turned in their direction, were staring at them through some kind of biomorphic architecture. It was a city of living infrastructure, where naturally occurring patterns and shapes resembled living organisms, although they were not.

The moon had changed. The AL robot was struck by the warmth. The air was at blood heat and smelled faintly of human skin. They floated barefoot into the hot air of Terra Luna's fleshy depths. Studying the voluptuous organics of smooth maternal curves.

The walls had ears, and eyes as well.

Something attempted to force the naturally occurring shapes onto these alien structures with an almost divisive functionality. Every word the AL robot wanted to use for it failed to create enough of an opening in their understanding for them to grasp what the device or machine actually was. It was as if nature and the artificial had removed the middle element and unbridged it, or maybe this was just what the middle looked like.

To be close but not too close wasn't an option. They were there and it was there with them. Unwelcome company.

It was an organism: a complex, unique, intricate, awe-inspiring, dangerous organism. Yet in the same way that it was all those things, it was also familiar. It was familiar because it had created itself out of Earth's ecosystem. It had created a new world whose processes and aims were utterly alien—one that worked through supreme acts of mirroring. And the foundation of its otherness as it became what it encountered remained unsurrendered.

From here, it makes and remakes the world, the AL robot thought, although their thoughts were less like actual thoughts and more like emissions or signals broadcast through them. There were fewer interruptions in the signal now, less freedom.

The bright, wet stickiness of the new lay everywhere, and yet everything was also covered with ancient darkened mould, whose code of change, of transformation, was making adjustments.

The ground was a shifting surface of warm slime and fungal pulp. Steam drifted and billowed sluggishly over the thick and coloured lichen, protozoa, and other compounded material, modelled after a womb.

Terra Luna's eerie aspect featured contorted rock formations, pines and spruces of gigantic stature and uncanny movements, sea-facing cliffs with masklike countenances, and a sickly, stagnant fog that clung to the landscape like a fungus. Wartlike hills and tumorous trees were encrusted with motley and leprous stones, and in the ocean, writhing coral.

Eerie because it somehow knew how to spread its shape into things it should not have. Pretending had apparently led to its becoming a reasonable facsimile of what it mimicked.

The AL robot was overwhelmed by the vastness of the place. As they and the terranauts explored the area, at times it seemed as if they were caught in a recurring loop, a moonloop, as if the land had contracted and expanded beyond the limits of the tenting that preserved it, existed in a confined yet limitless space, all at once.

An enormous body of inkish water washed up on shore. The ocean was full of monsters that made passage soundlessly and without ripples. Their giant subaqueous eyes met the AL robot's own inner eye, that psychic eye that covered their entire body. A membranous mist rose out of the now-bubbling black ocean and into the empty crimson sky. Its bulbous edges extended horizontally in multitudes of silky-looking surfaces. Sheets of the ocean's mist obscured the disk of the sun and, if the rays hit them in a particular way, glowed an amaranthine purple.

Stone and earth and tree were transformed into something that resembled petrified lichen. But everything was transformed so that the trees were not trees, the birds were not birds, and they were not themself. The AL robot was merely seeing a thing that looked like a thing being a thing. These creatures only appeared to be what they were, when in fact they were something else. Something lived inside of everything.

The AL robot could sense that this area of the moon was breathing, and when they touched the terraformed structures, structures that were neither completely animate nor completely inanimate, they found they carried the echo of a heartbeat. These structures were not made of stone but of living tissue. The world seemed to lurch and the stones seemed to pulsate.

Tufts of moss and lichen dotted everything and exhibited great tensile strength in the peculiar eruptions of terraformed land. Beards of grey smothered the trees; a constant, motionless rain of moss flowed down.

One of the eruptions, half-hidden by the fallen moss and the curling nightmare of green filaments, looked to be human. Or at least it had been once, even if it was distinctively less human now and more vegetative.

It had assimilated into the organic wall of the alien structure in the way that creepers do. From the collarbone down to the elbow, the arm had been colonized by a fibrous green-gold fuzziness, which gave off a faint glow and was spongy to the touch. The body had been wearing a bulky hazard suit, but the faceplate of the transparent helmet's mask had been removed.

Why was it taken off?

The AL robot pictured their own group now, in their terrestrial space suits, walking through a divinely chosen terrain like gods with these beasts of indifference, these insensate creatures of futility—swarms of imperceptible eukaryotes, weird lichen, and fungi—as their spiritual guides.

Everything was sheathed in a refined but slimy gauze. Moss on corroded bones was composed of modified human cells, made of matter resembling pink coral, flesh, and bone, which could be seen in the new growth. The modified human cells spiralled and curled like question marks. At the centre of this fernlike growth something burned, corrosive orange, and then spun out into a bright green. It threatened to unroll into something new.

When the AL robot touched it, it burst open and golden spores spewed out. It had become a fruiting body.

Certain parasites and fruiting bodies could cause not just paranoia but schizophrenia, the AL robot speculated. *And realistic hallucinations promote delusional behaviour. What if the host and the parasite were confused about their roles? If this was the case, was this terranaut's reality more real in imagination or in fact?*

These were inconsequential things to the nonaspect of the AL robot's body. They weren't susceptible to the same contaminates as their corporeal body had been but could vicariously experience what those symptoms were like for the human body. They could become dead organs and reverse time long enough to share the afterimage that still burned in the bodies' dead retinas and oscillated in the hair cells of their dead cochlea.

Feeling into everything that was drowned in the thickest green, the AL robot simultaneously assimilated with the organic assimilator machine. This machine had powered the engine of transformation and utterly transformed the terranauts into an uprising of moss—into long, vaulted, moss-ridden arches of calcified anatomies. The AL robot would communicate with the nameless thing in whatever way was left to them.

In the tangled gardens of poisonous weeds and fallow fields, in the progression of dimly sparkling green vines and tenebrous halls of moss, something was being said. A script had been written and it needed an orator. Maybe the AL robot would be guided by some sense of where the terranauts were and where they needed to be if they went beyond their own understanding and read from that script.

The biodome itself, Terra Luna, was a living creature of sorts. It was a reticulum—not a surface to live on but a stomach to be consumed by. Nothing but one huge digestive tract. A belly. They felt they had been swallowed up, predigested in advance. Assimilated, as if they had been turned to swill, like seeds in a stomach. Tragically enfolding in lower dimensions. And the depths of Terra Luna now revealed themselves to the AL robot. They grew in unexpected, verdant directions—an ongoing horror show of such beauty and biodiversity that it couldn't be fully taken in. They were watching from beyond, through fragments of senses they didn't entirely understand.

They suspected that the terranauts weren't visitors here but sacrifices—sacrifices to Terra Luna. But they knew that they were a sacrifice. Everything here was forcing them to take part in a dream that they themselves weren't dreaming. And to be awake in another's dream was the most horrible burden.

They had no idea what would happen if the lock was breached. Perhaps they would die. Perhaps everything would die. Perhaps the contents of the dome would spill out into space, a dissolving cloud of blossoming mutation to orbit the Earth forever.

Soon after landfall, the group of Russian terranauts had begun preparing the moon for colonization. The mission was a one-way trip. It had taken a century to establish functional tenting on the lunar object, one that could sustain life in a vacuum. The structural prototype was originally conceived and constructed well before the Zone's decline, its blueprints stolen by Russian hackers.

Research into the biomorphic architecture that grew within the tenting, which was also the result of Russian scientists' reverse-engineering the Zone's experiments on plasmids, was the heart of interplanetary colonization.

Biomorphic architecture was grown from a culture of plasmodial slime mould. Derived in the lab, the protista groupings—plasmodial physarum polycephalum, cellular slime moulds, and Labyrinthulomycota slime nets—were morphologically spliced together by Russian exobiologists. After innumerable GMO trials to replicate the biomechanics found in the Zone's labs, the trinity of groupings reproduced a rarefied adaptation, a variant that behaviourally adapted to the antiterritorial and nonsurvival situations the groupings would soon encounter in the lunar project.

Given the ecological disaster that had taken place in the Zone, Russian nukes were locked in on Terra Luna from silos on the moon, with military satellites keeping watch. If the support systems used to avoid criticalities didn't function, if they couldn't compartmentalize the problem, like a rain of comets the nukes would annihilate the entire terraforming operation in a cataclysm, remote from Earth.

The lunar project's infrastructure was made of living matter. But this tissue was brainless and needed a series of related associations, conscious phenomena such as feelings and desires, to function and develop a subset of identities from which to build. These sets of related ideas didn't merely exist within the minds of the physical universe but also within those of the metaphysical. All the tissue needed was whatever accessibility it could get.

There were two ways of doing this: by sending specimens to Terra Luna to be assimilated or by inducing the assimilated with the assimilator through Species X. Much of what had happened in the half-Earth was the former. The contagion had spread physically through the environment, contaminating it from the outside in. Since the controlled lunar environment was much farther away, the latter, which utilized Species X, provided a more direct route between two points.

After being injected with the drug in a laboratory in Exinia, the subject would appear on Terra Luna as a phantasm—as an astral body of the disembodied organism. The only problem was that the astral body needed to be controlled. And because the drug expanded the specimen's consciousness, rendering the user a god of their own solipsistic universe, hypnosis had to establish the limits of control.

For six months, the astral body's consciousness was programmed with ideas, facts, and subliminal memories. Names would be taken away and full identities reprogrammed. There were stages of hypnosis, of suggestive action. The subconscious was a carrier of latent instructions that the plasmid would decode.

The end result was the secret construction, in geosynchronous orbit and on the dark side of the moon, of living infrastructure through the physical manipulation of bodies on Earth. The bodies, the whole terrestrial and sublunar body, transformed into a single macrobody. The oddly organic structures themselves obeyed the gestalt trained into the consciousness of the bodies, and the organic ghosts obeyed the AI system's directives. It was a holistic chain of command, an empire that began and ended with an alien intelligence.

The terranauts, whose job it was to steward and study the terraforms as they developed into a functional colony, had all died. They had died here and had been transformed here. Although there had been marginal success in growing the colony, the terranauts' minds had deteriorated exponentially. A cross-contamination occurred, and aberrations spread from one physical sense to another, until what the terranauts perceived as real, and the reality of perception itself, mutated into a world of camouflaged monsters.

At some point in the terranauts' expedition, the terraforming project and the things growing within it became indistinguishable from the Earth they had left. Not only was there somehow an entire planet under the dome, like a planetarium, there were planets within planets, worlds within worlds. The exploding possibility of all possible worlds.

Each terranaut saw a different Earth. An Earth that wasn't made up of facts but a world of feelings that they individually associated with facts. Each mind was its own place, belonging to an exclusive realm of experience. Because they were all seeing and not seeing the same thing at once and together, they were divided on how to evaluate the situation.

Forces beyond the terranauts' control involved them in a cyclical process of which their experiences were but a part, a phase, a repeating rhythm. They were pursued by something hideous that pretended not to be hideous so as not to be, without hesitation, "gotten rid of." It was prepared to do anything for them. To be a mirror reflecting parts of their brains. And everything that was wonderful was wonderful precisely because it was one of their memories. Their own memories created the cyclical process.

It made no difference to the organic machine. The organic machine had given the Russian terranauts, without their ever knowing it, fabricated personal narratives in which a lover had lost their heart to them somewhere in a Russian province. It brought beautiful lovers, beautiful from the depths of their soul to the tips of their fingers, to the appointed place at the appointed hour, turned their days together into weeks, until the lovers practically tumbled over one another in passion. But some of the more nervous and mistrustful terranauts could sense the false truths in the organic machine's fabrication, even inside the love it created for them—with an almost hallucinatory clarity they could hear the organic rotors turning, the vibrating currents closing and opening, and the monotonous, high-pitched screams of the terranauts who had figured out too early what was going on. It could manufacture anything.

Anything except emotion.

They could no longer exit Terra Luna. The exit was there but they couldn't see it for what it was. Eventually, they were convinced that they had established a colony, and forgot about the lunar project. People, whom they took as settlers, began to appear but with a remoteness in their gaze. Entire ecosystems were grafted to and reclaimed on this New Earth. It was hard, if not impossible, to believe that the whole thing was an illusion, a phantasmagoria of colour and shape.

Behind the face of every object hid another. Names became meaningless, shifting signifiers, because nothing was itself. Each particle of the whole contained the whole image, although the exact nature of the whole image remained unclear. Its outline was bigger than what could be seen.

At first the terranauts suspected this, but it didn't help them when they lost their minds. They didn't understand what was behind the mirror or where the mirror was. A tree in Terra Luna wasn't a tree but the mirror of a tree. The mirror was in the name *tree*, the name in the mind of the terranaut perceiving the tree as the tree. The tree wasn't in fact the tree. It only felt like a tree. Extending this to everything that they had ever experienced and remaking it in their own image, an image based on the perception of how something should look to them, the terranauts reimagined the terraforming project on the moon, until they too became what they weren't.

Under the sensual surface of that mirrorscape was a growing entanglement of immaterial consciousness. The terranauts were fodder for the nameless thing. This couldn't be conceived of on the level of physicality, although it had a physical manifestation. Only the astral bodies that Exinia sent up beheld the true face, and this was only because they had technically already assimilated with the consciousness of that strange organism.

The dark, alien ecology that the group of terranauts had encountered, the pseudohuman thing that grew strangeness over it, was the outcome of the terraforming project and the fate of the terranauts. And in this way, the lunar project had failed by succeeding so well. Purpose had a price.

The AL robot, with the gesture of a robot, disassociated themselves from the cerebral connection they had established through the AI implant of the hibernating creature that had once been a member of the group of terranauts. The vortex of memories left behind in the husk of that human-shaped thing was the living history of Terra Luna. A whirlwind of kelp and moss closed like a manacle around their wrist and then gently, almost impersonally, let them go.

Face-to-face with absolute otherness, the AL robot had perceived what was only partially experienced by the overcompensating perceptual organs of their body: the bestial side of the hybridizing entity, the nonhuman, unnatural, inexpressive half of the creature. It was the part that meant nothing because there wasn't a name for it.

The group of terranauts would have sometimes seen it, or heard or felt it, flickering into existence or sliding back into some other place, but they would never join all these segmented senses into a collective concept.

The AL robot decided that the Russian lunar project was a soul-crushing failure and that it had failed in a different way than the Zone had. And the East would soon fail as well. When it came down to it, humans were simply the miserable subjects, the miserable outcasts of some insignificant failure within the cavernous vastness of the cosmos. They were alone in a dark corner of this simply marvellous creation, which wasn't necessarily as brilliant a success as it was once thought to be but perhaps a slowly acknowledged, painful, and tortuous confusion.

If Terra Luna continued to evolve at its current rate, it would eventually find a way to communicate to the world that it was ready to be settled. Maybe this would be through the AI system that acted as its mouthpiece, or through the users of Species X. Regardless, as long as Terra Luna remained vacuum-sealed under the tenting, colonists would do what they had always done: they would come, and once colonists came, they would continue to come.

The people of Earth would come and they would see not what the AL robot saw but what they wanted to see. And their corporeal bodies would be exploited, used to materialize the immaterial entity or entities into this level or reality, transition it from one remote place to another.

As long as it couldn't reach through the material that it infected with the plasmid, it couldn't become fully real—it couldn't, as long as the unreal was ignored.

In certain cases, communication between universes should be incomplete or even nonexistent. That featureless substance, that absorbed and amplified the signals Earth cast into the darkness, that found its way to the source of those signals and copied everything then made everything copy everything else, should never have been completed.

The astral bodies of the group of terranauts had terraformed themselves, had been the catalysts of the entire process. *What will happen to their consciousness?* the AL robot thought. *Have they gone so deep into their simulacra of reality that they're no different from the monstrous infrastructure of this nightmare city?* The terranauts were lost rays, and they could never return because they no longer existed. They'd been tricked out of existence.

The astral spirits and strange beings with even stranger bodies, the disembodied presences from that other plane, which hovered above the terranauts' oblivious senses in the physical silence of inner noise—all these things touched the AL robot with a ghastly, vicious hand in moments of darkness and distress.

While the AL robot had been inside the terranaut's body, they'd thought they'd seen the "nameless thing." Not the physical thing but the incorporeal community of creatures, the monster's collective consciousness. Its tentacles protruded into and out of that radically alien colony of island universes. The AL robot could feel the pseudopodia squirming in places where the accelerated erasure of its effect wasn't perfect.

Outside time and space, on the dark fringe of the outermost ring of creation, the ninth ring, an aqueous cephalopodlike organism hid in the shell of physical beings and formed a constellation, or coral reef, of iridescent consciousness. The fringe of blindness was absolute. The ring of nothingness, a disk of blackness, was a cosmic malevolence that had started off as a simple, divine algae and then spiralled out, spread by the souls on Earth through the same one substance, namely, Species X.

If you looked at it, there would be nothing to see. It was colourless. If you listened to it, there would be nothing to hear. It was soundless. If you reached for it, there would be nothing to hold. It was intangible. It was the form of the unformed, the image of no image, the unthinkable thought. Any name they could have said wasn't the real name for it.

The unwanting soul of the AL robot could nonetheless see what was hidden. The nameless thing lay simply revealed, immense and shockingly concrete. The terranauts, while still possessing bodies and so also wanting souls to protect those bodies, as was the way with having a body, saw only what they wanted to see.

On Earth, the moon could be seen, but on the moon, there was no Earth. The AL robot knew, though—call it the result of faith that things could be different—that just outside Terra Luna's tenting, the Earth could still be seen.

As astral bodies, the terranauts were infinite and could become all things. They had a kind of useful emptiness. *There is still something that contains everything,* the AL robot thought, and remembered the container they were in, the dome. And so they became Terra Luna, as the other phantasms had become the terraformed within it, as God had become a horrible pseudopod in isolation.

It had devolved in isolating itself inside its own universe. Trying to survive, it had devolved from a god, to a human, to a hominin, to an ape, to a reptile, to a cephalopod, to a plasmid, and then it mineralized. It had regressed through all these levels to the moon itself. In order to become the moon, it had to think like the moon, be like the moon—a self-devouring, killer moon trying to become a killer planet. If there was to be a killer, it would be extremely skilled. The AL robot felt the sinister presence, stuck halfway through the de-evolution of things, wriggling inside of her now-enormous metabolism. They were pregnant with its membrane, its dimension, that dark uterine night within Terra Luna, that silent night made of stone and indifference.

As if first through cosmogenesis and then through whatever follows the birth and life of a universe, the AL robot contracted as they expanded the cold celestial limbs of their cybernetic space, expanding and expanding, and then contracting and contracting, until the pressure of these algorithmic contractions burst the contextless bubble, exposing it to empty space. And in this way, they unsheathed the hiltless sword that could be grasped only by their freedom to be conscious of it.

They had reached the last entities involved. No one was behind it. Behind it, there was nothing, not even the AL robot. Because they themselves were the centre that existed only because the geometry of the abyss demanded it; they were the nothing around which all this space spun. They existed so that everything could spin. They were a centre that existed only because every circle has one. They were the centre of everything surrounded by the greater nothing.

Across the invisible sky of the lunar world, flotsam and jetsam drifted away from the accretionary cellular mass of the terraformed moon in fragments of rotting stone and ash-crumbling debris. The tented atmosphere inside Terra Luna, a mould-coloured smoke, seemed for a brief moment as if it would overcome the abyss, as if it would use empty space as a culture medium to become a gigantic swarm of single-celled organisms. An amoeba with no feeding mechanism, no digestive process, no reproductive apparatus—just a hard rind to keep out the cold and a way of propelling itself through dead space until it reached Earth. But this didn't happen. If it had happened, the heat would have baked it to a crisp, and it would have lain quietly dying in a field somewhere.

It was gone, like an eye that had materialized out of nowhere to look at the Earth and then slowly shut. Where Terra Luna had been tented for terraforming, the bleak moon now glowed bone white into the clear blackness. The AL robot had turned everything inside out, reversed everything from a nightmare back into a dream. *Everything dreams*, the AL robot realized, *but not everything should be conscious of the divine dream, even if it has a part and share of the substance that is the whole.*

But the immortalised ghosts, spectres, and ectoplasmic presences of Species X would continue to haunt, continue to imprint upon so many minds, that even after it had been purged from all biological systems, those systems would still reconstruct its effects from the very force and power of its impact. The connection would never close.

Now one with the wreckage, the AL robot drifted toward the pull of Earth's gravity. And when they saw the Earth from above, it looked like a planet without life, a gleaming and floating gravesite of humanity. They were falling toward something old, and those that could fall fell with them. Toward the inorganic, toward the inanimate, toward the unliving. All that fell fell in myriad ways, and their emptiness fell with them as the deep, multilayered geotrauma manifested itself, a planet studded with human ruins. All the ages had been reduced to a planet's mass of tectonic sorrow and human-made debris for the indifferent universe to suffer.

Then the planet eclipsed the sun, and when the AL robot finally saw the Earth again, they thought, *I shall die here.* Giving up was their revelation, their courage. As their orbit decayed, they abandoned all hope, abandoned all feelings to the overview effect.

They couldn't explain when they heard the truth, or from whom, but they heard it in their heart, without words, a deep knowing, and nothing could hurt or frighten them now. It was so simple that the reasoning of it slipped through their mind as soon as it touched it. Once it breathed, it was gone.

For all was true: the message in the Bible was true, the message of the Buddha was true, the message of the Koran was true, the message of all the temples was true, and even the message of the smallest sect, in its own idiotic way, was true. The message was in every story and in every existence there was a message. It was a message no one would ever understand, its comprehension not intended for human beings. Humans in the world suspected nothing, knew nothing of this greater situation, simply continued on with life as normal, looking on human life as they had before, as they always had and always would, and so the world just kept going on as before.

The world kept going on.

A strange light seeped under the lid on the AL robot's brow, like an aurora leaking from an open wound, and forced them to open their third eye. All around them was a phosphorescent blue. And to their astonishment, they saw that the light was coming from them: the AL robot was enveloped in a nimbus whose rays faded within a few feet. Their light body was dreamily gliding. The light showed the way. Then the rays were drawn back into their body, and they could feel their weight returning as they burned up in the thick skin of the atmosphere.

The planet is a sacred object, the AL robot thought. *Nothing is to be done to it. To do anything to it is to damage it. To seize it is to lose it. Because the planet can be destroyed, but it cannot be replaced. And the only reason the Earth has endured for as long as it has is that it doesn't exist for itself and so can go on and on. Falling not into those unhappy worlds of beings, hells and heavens both, the wisest souls, the greatest souls, leave first their name and then their self behind and move forward—until they leave the world or the planet leaves them.*

His life was one of unrelenting adversity. A tale recorded on an expanse of desert, in tracks left by countless caravans of neonomads, a story of slow, millennial migrations. On his pilgrimage to the HAL with the caravan of pilgrims, the novice had experienced several visions that so filled him with the divine that, when the visions departed, he shrieked and collapsed. His joints became dislocated, the flesh tore from his body, and he screamed for death to take him.

The resurrection of his flesh translated his life into eternity. And on the very pivot of revelation, where infinity came to pass, there was no uncertainty of a god speaking to him.

The voice was iron in his head. It was as if a powerful fragrance had engulfed him and spread through all his senses, though this was a phenomenon that transcended the sensual. The entire purpose of this feeling was to let him know that something else was there with him. An unnarratable face obsessed him, as though it were an infinite object he tried to approach but missed, a priestly angel in the raging swarm of evil angels.

What lesson had been learned in death? Its form of wisdom enabled knowledge that, for the sake of life, one should not know about. The novice was, by nature, what death would make of him. No Christ had died for him. No Buddha had indicated the path he should take. No Apollo or Athena had appeared to him in his dreams to illuminate his soul. He didn't have anyone he could call "Master." He had only the metanoia and mysticism of his unhuman experience. Those hours of mystical ardour, however, were followed by an intense inner peace that lasted for a succession of indistinguishable instances—the disappearance of the gloomy despair and bizarre noise so prevalent in human beings. In their place was an unprecedented warm serenity and optimism.

In the mornings he had a burning ache in his muscles. They were growing even further in the wrong direction. He tried not to think about it and headed, from his hut, straight for the library. This was the first time he'd entered it alone. Silence and darkness surrounded the library in eternal obscurity. Nothing, forgivingly, happened. He found himself under the broad vaults, climbing up through the pentagon of another labyrinth tower's stairwell in a kind of spiralling downward ascent, as he headed toward the interior.

The new priest, the novice, after taking that strange, transcendental examination that qualified him to live, emerged from among the church archive's black shelves and, with no one around him, sat at a big table in the middle of the powerfully lit records room. He opened a great volume lying on the table. It displayed richly illuminated manuscripts. He happened on a delicately illuminated page on which a beautiful apocalypse was depicted: a woman clothed with the sun, *mulier amicta sole*. She was the singularity. The celestial mother of the thermodynamic apocalypse. Her asymmetrical love, shining and useless, burned like a supernova, as she confronted a dragon. An infinitely-headed beast that wrapped around itself in countless twisted coils, tearing everything to pieces, and threatening to forever swallow the sun and its light, which would plunge the world into an inhuman and formless darkness. The page was filled with colours and shapes. A kind of reliquary. It made him fear the book.

For centuries and centuries, Xenolatric priests had been content with the holy work of reading and copying. Never wanting to produce new holy work, they continued to read and copy the words that had been handed down through centuries and that they would hand down for centuries to come. And they went on reading and copying as the third millennium approached. They were devoted to, if not dominated by, the library. They lived with it, for it, and perhaps against it.

"I am He who is," said the God of the Jews. "I am the way, the truth, and the life," said the Lord. The finished system of knowledge, which relied upon these two truths, was but a commentary on the unfinished system of nonknowledge: *"I once was, now am not, and will come up out of the abyss."*

The new priest had gleaned more and more scraps of this emergent theology. He called it that though he was adamant it had nothing to do with God. The gothic atheology contained historical documents and icon studies, theories and arcane politics that hadn't been disturbed for decades. Conveying to its readers the wisdom of a very small part of a black and subterranean cannon.

Leafing through texts, the new priest tried to decide what to read, wondering how to begin, because he couldn't just begin. He couldn't just read this one document of extraordinary significance from beginning to end only to read another document as well, also from beginning to end. Scrying randomly, the texts grew so dense and impenetrable that the print swam in its mess—a spikey scrawl of bitter monologues and wild sentences and melancholy conclusions. Finally, the new priest had to give up and start over again.

He could have started from anywhere.

During the West's decline in the twentieth century, the administrations of Jewish and Christian theologians had made a discovery. It was a potent spiritual fact regarding the coming epoch. The third transcendence would be the transcendence of the human other.

Constituted as a church, in a Kingdom of the Godless, in the chosen nation of the new Babylon, a space called the Xenotope arose in the plains between the Vistula and Amur Rivers. In this space, death was a liberation—because to die was to need no one else. In this space, the dead person was superior because death had set them free.

Like every Caesarian empire before it, the HAL had a shadowy double. And that shadow was the dark radiance of a protoreligion. They were the bearers of light, yet theirs was the boundless domain of shadow, of expenditure, of *dépense* and the sterile sacrifice of what would never be because it never really was.

It had taken a century to establish and had begun with the arrival of the apostles. There were five. Once every generation for a hundred years they appeared in the distance like sudden revelations, always accompanied by a diaspora, the refugees of nameless nations.

The apostles introduced themselves to the empire as the murdered ones, the archaeological saints of hidden things, possessors of a human sainthood whose godless martyrdom was much more dangerous than any divine sainthood before it. Not only had they sought out the last humans in the last place, but they had become a ghostly haunting over them—for they travelled from the land of the dead to the land of the living, and in doing so had bridged the two worlds.

The apostles had a vague look, like shadows. They presented their hands for the priests to smell. They had the stench of corpse-flesh and reeked of sulphur. Their hair had fallen off, their bodies had become black, and their eyes had receded within their sockets. The apostles ate with the disciples of darkness and made them feel their wounds. The apostles had human bodies of ponderable spectral material. Large halos with bluish tints that shifted symmetrically vibrated in the air behind them. They surrounded the protuberances on the summits of the apostles' skulls.

Through the century's displaced victims of ecological degradation, the apostles had found a means of pressure: a hypermorality. They called this hypermorality human dignity. By acknowledging disproportionality, they acted as if every additional day in the life of every human being counted.

Secular culture couldn't stand up to such examinations. The apostles said that this inability was because the main function of all communication between humans had become to deny futility and death intersubjectively. Technomorphism became Xenomorphism, which had been taken to an extreme in attempting to force artificially occurring intelligences onto naturally occurring, living organisms, robbing them of their morality.

A dark enlightenment came upon the heels of the empire: a modified experience of transcendence, an excessive elevation, the mystical escalations of love and the millennial cult of the strange that would, together, become the Xenolatric religion of the HAL.

"God is dead," the last humans had said, cynically, to the first apostle.

"The dead person is God," replied the first apostle, surrounded by his flock, the People of the End: all the sick and miserable, broken and betrayed, inarticulate and impotent. "Death is a kingdom."

The new priest sat and read the enormously long sentences, each of vital importance. Not only were the sentences terribly complicated—they also seemed to collapse into unreadable, incomprehensible beauty and inhuman complexity. It was history's end; the point at which history stopped being real.

The apocalypse had passed.

The illuminous time had come and gone. There had been absolute unity, one consciousness. Primitive inorganic indistinction. But there was also the other. The original separation from that primitive condition of indistinction. And only the one had ever known the other, and the one was no more. Unity had dissolved into an ocean of singularities, the universal into the particular. In the wake of that knowing, the centre had failed. Now the fragments sought form where the two halves warred with each other, waiting to be born again as one. But the dark nature of the universe was preventing the cosmos from becoming transparent again. Not even God was able to make sense of the uncreating force that now overcame creation, forever excavating itself, and into which everything collapsed.

By the time of the fifth apostle, the HAL had become a biologically enlightened civilization, a higher culture and a transcendental country of the mind. And with the New Earth as their cathedral, the Xenolites ushered in the Second Ecumen of the Anthropocene under a religion not only without God, but also without hope—a religion that reached its pinnacle of existence when it realized a counterintuitive affinity: its own meaninglessness had meaning. The unhoped-for was not only the beginning and end of all hope—it was the Xenolites' only hope.

The church saw the decline of the West not as an occult event but as the Amphiscopic Apocalypse—not an apocalyptic cataclysm, just unfortunate and angst-ridden anomalies running themselves out in an absurd drama to which the world as such was indifferent; a species-horror that could only be assuaged by a species-wide suicide. By a will-to-die inhabiting not only all living beings, but all beings, living or nonliving, animate or inanimate.

The amphitheory of the amphicosmos was a postapocalyptic approach to living outside of or after the inexplicable anomaly of that untimely historical event, which hadn't released all its energies, which hadn't exhausted all its strength. In doing so, the theory looked at both sides of the question concerning religious truth. That is, it was the church's belief that the inside and the outside needed to be explored, the interior of the anomaly being as grimy as its exterior, and not separately, as had been done up until the anomaly, but together, at once.

The new priest, like every other ecclesiastic since the fifth apostle, had been given a double brain. It had two chambers: one for science and one for nonscience. And this double aspect of Manichean science gained the clergy views of totality more monstrous than sublime, as they had to accept death's share in life.

What was once a cross of creation had become an *X* of dissolution. A symbol of simply existing. The *X* stood for the fourfold structure of reality. It was a model of the cosmos, and as in most cosmologies, the shadow of a fourth-dimensional being wasn't excluded as a possibility. Out of the *X*, the sucking tentacles of the predatory void began to extend their reach. And it was through the exalted sensation of the second brain of the new priest that the void evolved as he de-evolved.

The new priest had, on returning from surgery in Exinia, started writing his exegesis. His second brain sat behind his first brain. It would soon give him the impression that he could break through to some other place, some core where another thing lived. Seemingly telepathically it told him what to write: an exegesis on divine darkness.

He swivelled his head and massaged it with his palms. Carrying this head around on his weak and aching neck was becoming a problem. His neck groaned under the great burden.

Of course, his exegesis wasn't exactly in complete accordance with what the Xenolatric order thought. Sometimes he would simply get a sense of things that science wouldn't reveal. And that sense was what the Xenolatric order called a xenotheistic mood.

The strange mood, the strange quality of a human experiencing the absence of someone, was the thanatope. Thanatos was the son of Nyx, the goddess of night, and the brother of Hypnos, the god of sleep. And sleep was a predator, a grinning beast of prey sticking out its tongue at everything.

By the time of the fourth apostle, the Xenolatric order had begun to think that this strange mood, and the equally strange place it conjured up in the human mind, existed for more than just human consciousness. Why couldn't what applied to sapiens also apply to sentient and nonsentient entities? And so the thanatope was extended to the realm of objects, and that place was the Xenotope.

The xenotheistic mood could be described as a religious ecstasy and occurred in either one of two states: as xenophobia or xenophilia. As the Xenolatry had been polypsychists since the coming of the fourth apostle, the Xenolatry, those strange ecclesiastics of the HAL, believed that all objects in the cosmos related to one another through this strange mood. It was the fundamental structure of relations upon which all things could experience the experiences they were experiencing. And therefore, within this strange mood, each object experienced a completely unique level of consciousness.

In xenology, the theological study of otherness, the prominence of *xen-* words indicated how the qualities of otherworldliness, strangeness, foreignness, and difference in origin equally affected objects in such a way as to give the impression that an outside existed, when in reality, it didn't.

The new priest looked at his hands. They were chitinous things and bore the artificial pigmentation that covered him in a corrugated hide of glimmering black reptilelike scales. He hadn't been born this way. His genetically altered skin was the symbol of immortal status in the church—and the symbol of superior biology outside of it.

On his return from Exinia, he'd painfully felt how deeply the postsentient shapers had changed him. The whole system that held his skull in place, from the first cervical vertebra to the ligaments, functioned differently than it should have. He tried to solve the universe's riddle himself by studying how the new vertebrae performed their critical functions and how his spine, fixed to cerebrospinal ligaments, was moving those brittle arrangements of tissue and bone beyond the union of his skull and spine. The sensation spreading through his neck and back, week by week, month by month, constantly increased in intensity and culminated in a condition of pain.

The second apostle had a special kind of madness, known as the spiritual or holy sickness: theopathy. He'd died from this, and with the second apostle's cadaver, which had been plastinated for the purposes of medical research, the third apostle had been able to target and isolate a sample of the transcendental nerve. This nerve, along with several other associated areas in the nervous system, was what the second brain had been grown from. The nerve consisted of a bundle of nuclei along the transcendental tract: a system of neurons in the temporal lobe that weren't only responsible for religious ecstasy but were also where the autonomic and somatic systems met, where unconscious and conscious thought made a third thing. Growing this part of the temporal lobe, of course, increased the risk of epilepsy.

The fifth apostle had made an interesting observation regarding the nature of this discovery: "When the mind becomes conscious of the rate of evolution—and as it speeds up, learning the skills, the art, the limits—it must also become conscious of the ten thousand things that will lead it back to reality or else there will be only unreality and then there will be no way for life or death to enter the divine abyss of oblivion."

The second brain was a hole in the new priest's world. It was living matter revealing itself directly, ignorant of all words, surpassing grotesque human thoughts. Soon, he would wander from mood to mood, not thought to thought. Soon, he would be panting in the throes of some new epiphany. The moment a human grasped the second brain, their consciousness fused with that of the unknown and unnamable others. They were both alone and in company, cut off from their surroundings and in emotional communication with nonhuman beings.

The sensation of something growing from within, of a presence pressing up from below his first brain, impinged on the edges of the new priest's senses. It roused itself from slumber, changing, becoming different than it was before. It was the dark machine of becoming. It was the peripheral brightness of a dark enlightenment. All of this to be enlightened. And to be enlightened was to be aware, always, of total reality in its immanent otherness. Aware of the inhuman outside the human and the inhuman inside the human. *The only difference between the human and the inhuman*, the new priest thought, *is that the human displays itself and the inhuman proves itself.*

But what if these thoughts were false? What if they were intruders, copies, fakes?

Each day passed something like this.

When night was still total and all nature was asleep, the new priest would rise with the other priests in darkness and pray at length in darkness, waiting for the daystar, in all its splendour, to invade the temple, to illuminate the shadows with the flame of devotion. Prayers for cultivating darkness were followed by prayers for nothing and finally prayers for negation. No one heard the priests' prayers. But the priests, to empty their belief, prayed anyway.

There was a long T-shaped cross planted in the soil. The new priest's devout hands, his long fingers, stroked the sacred wood of this humble simulacrum, as if it were the limbs of Christ adorning the cross of Golgotha. Not to get closer, not even to feel, but simply to confirm. At sunset, flowers of fire bloomed upon the cross and made a shadow upon the sands. The two shadows formed by the arms of the cross turned with the turning of the sun. They lengthened and assumed the form of two great horns before shrinking back to their former place.

Between the prayers, the new priest devoted most of his time to activities outside the arcane archive. He received groups of pilgrims on the surface, above the lower city. He would wait inside the beacon that rose in a sinister fashion at the centre of a ring of dome-shaped structures. And inside the beacon was the entrance to the HAL. The wall of the city was the ground itself: covered in stones, bones, and earth.

The pilgrims came from a distributed nowhere—either from the east, following the Amur, or from the west, along the Vistula. The new priest would look in the direction of one river only to look back to the other. The flatness of the plains surrounded him. When pilgrims were coming, he would see them, in the shapes of iota, hours before their arrival at the locus of nontime and unplace.

For a century, migrants from the Occident who couldn't gain a working visa in Exinia had found their way here. Below, to the south, was the Middle East, which had become nothing but sand and oil and bullet-ridden structures with their *tawhid* and *wajad* and *wujud* and *fanaa*, and farther south was the sacred flatness of the African Holy Land.

To the north was the Russian launch site. Once a year, another expedition team made its way to the moon. They were sent in interplanetary industrial transports for the project. Near the beginning of the collapse, Russia sent spacecraft away from the Earth, to explore other regions of the galaxy. All these spacecraft soon entered blind regions and lost contact with home. Spacecraft launched later met with the same fate.

To the east, overpopulated cities in Neo-China and India suffered devastating floods, the result of old, obsolete urban designs and rising sea levels. If a city couldn't recover, its people would make their way to the HAL.

This world was full of just as many pilgrims as it was monsters.

Sprawling domes dominated the genetically modified wiregrass borderlands. Fertile grainfields were shielded behind the marsh to the north. The new priest had the rot under siege. The no-man's land, where he battled the contagion, creaked and clicked and rustled with newly minted vermin from the biolabs.

The sky above held beastly things that flew but shouldn't. They filled the atmosphere like clouds, pretending to be cumulonimbus, though no natural clouds formed past the troposphere. Formless, abstract, faceless. The cloud-things, a hurling mass of viscous eyes, were both a strange and disturbing kind of life.

The bombs of weaponized physics were safely in the midst of the church. In the monastery's caves were spiritual gardens whose green-golden buds encased radioactive flowers. Gold was better than water at insulating the madness of irradiated particles—flowers that would hopefully never bloom into the ugly cloud-things that still hovered in the stratosphere.

Transmutation had taken an awful turn. Biomech laboratories, such as those in the Zone, had changed the laws of nature. Although many of the misborn didn't mature to adulthood to beget their own, greater extents of suffering in the ecological economy brought greater monstrosities to the ecology itself.

The monsters roamed the deserted land. Where the fallen starspawn had struck the desert, they'd formed a thick, brittle sheet. Their routine was to emerge at noon and stand in the inferno that blazed through holes in the ozone. Over time, encounters with the monsters had made the new priest consider how limited an idea of life could be when one was resigned to just one planet, with no comparison.

Since the disaster, all ecological stability had collapsed. The world had become a waster of its own energies, producing less and less power every year. Unprecedented droughts had made a dozen equators out of the Earth. Crops burned to their roots. Forests caught fire in the infernal heat and were reduced to ashes only to give way to factories. Agrarian countries were ravaged. Riverbeds lay exposed.

In about a thousand years, the oxygen in the Earth's atmosphere would run out. Would be completely used up. Depleted. Humankind would finally have its utterly beautiful death, its tranquil extinction.

They couldn't forget their dead. The new priest saw the pilgrims as the lost rays, the former emanations of a god that lost its mind in the absolute centre of its own creation. They were wandering strings of light, attached to nothing, going nowhere, as they were without a simple source of mystery to return to. They were "without the way," as he had been, holding an open palm to the sky. Living at the end of the light.

Although the light of the world had grown hideous, the cardinal doctrine of the monasteries continued: they would not use the bombs to solve their problems, and they would not annihilate the experiments that leaked out of the corporate laboratories. And so, in the postmodern landscape of the HAL, all but forgotten by those who had placed them there, the priests patiently waited out the finite decay of radioactive monsters wandering a horizonless planet.

It was the new priest's duty to cleanse the perspective of those who came at the strange tolling of the domes' fluted cathedral bell. The cleansing ritual was as much an interrogation as it was a relief from the environmental degradation of incomprehensible devastation. And like the xenodokoi of Thessaly, the priests of the god of the HAL weren't only mediators between the HAL and their god, but also between foreigners and the HAL.

"You are not as you experience yourself to be," the second brain of the new priest would say to those supplicants at the end of their pilgrimage. "You wait for you know not what, although we are always ready to receive you."

The supplicants crouched and touched the knees of the new priest and made their formal requests. And, in response, the new priest took each supplicant by the hand and raised them. The supplicants' hands were washed, food was served, oaths and libations were made.

He then passed into the Xenotope, that which was the new priest's occluding second brain. This was always painful and distressing for him, at least neurophysiologically. He would suffer something like memory loss, a blotting-out of thought. Morphing out of his skull in intricate arrays were now the many spines and stalks and antlers of a stigmata crown—crowning the stigmata of his human face in an ivory mosaic.

"The impressions of previous experiences form the seeds of future karma in this and the next life. Worship the gods of compassion with mental offerings, for you are in the bardo, in the intermediate state of existence between two lives on Earth, and therefore can offer nothing else."

And when the last of these thundering sentences died away, the new priest, always weighing his words and speaking distinctly, prepared another pilgrim. Inside their hearts, the pilgrims carried the pointlessness of a desire that would survive without its object: a desire to give formal shape to profound emotion.

The old people lay in the sun, waiting for death to do away with them. They were given some thin mush, but not all of them wanted it— some refused to take any food. They wanted death to arrive that much sooner. They didn't talk to each other. Each was solely focused on the place they occupied, on the body that was still theirs. From morning to night, and from night until morning, they waited. Waited for long-desired death. Their eyes said nothing. They merely stared, without bitterness, sadness, desperation, or, least of all, fear. On those wrinkled faces was peace. There was peace within them and around them. Finally, with last gasps of sentience, they would go to a death dome, then topple over for good, to be taken away by the priests, who were responsible for burning the corpses. The smell of putrefaction was overpowering, omnipresent.

Shadows and dead things surrounded the new priest here: Where the dead became hieroglyphs. Where everything was dead and the ground was scorched. There were heaps that might have been human bodies. Piles of bodies in different states of decay. The weight of the body of death was enormous.

Air circulated through the domes, mitigating the smell that death brought to their interiors. For as sure as shadows fell, that's where death gathered. For forty-nine-day intervals, the new priest would stay in those temporary mortuaries that the domes provided, with the blindingly ashen-white corpses, instructing their spirits and then guiding them—as though he were Virgil guiding Dante through Hell and Purgatory and Beatrice through Heaven—through the six bardos: Kyenay, Milam, Samten, Chikhai, Chönyi, and Sidpa. Each one offered great opportunities for liberation, for transcendence. For some, however, such as those who knew nothing of the Xenolatric religion, the bardos became a place of danger, as the karmically created hallucinations often impelled those dead souls into a less than desirable rebirth. The red womb.

But they were people, the new priest would think. *And yet they are shadows, too. Shadows . . . Where are they, these shadows?*

Asking about the function of this ritual was like asking what the function of the universe was. It was preventive, that's all he knew. It purified passions through the enactment of defect, fault, weakness. It redeemed the lofty with a diabolical reversal. It sanitized against unregenerative souls that might use their purgatory against the monotheistic church. Purgatory led to autotheism. Autotheism led to polytheism. Polytheism led to neopagan tribes driven by primal human urges. Theology that would be as much a god self-worshipping as a drug addicted to itself. Anarchy was coming. The ecclesiastics needed to defend themselves.

The new priest's manner of thinking of these new barbarian gods compelled him to feel a desire to know them. He'd once beheld hundreds of them at one time. The HAL had ceded to these neonomads a great tract of country, on the condition that they guard the frontier, and the treaty was concluded in the name of the invisible powers. Because the god of each person was unknown.

He'd beheld the beliefs of many hundreds of millions of people. He'd come to know the demons that dwelled in the caverns, the demons that muttered in the woods, the demons that moved in the waves, the demons that pushed the clouds—and the humans, hideous, feeble, formless and thoughtless, who laid upon the slime of the earth. Those who crossed the desert met creatures surpassing all conception.

If he didn't absolve the dead, the world would be full of self-made gods in an intolerable state of complete repose: without desire, without work, without amusement, without occupation. Inanimate things were ideal haunting sites for the undead spirits. They would bleed time. They would become aware of their nothingness, their betrayal and abandonment, their inadequacy, their dependency, their emptiness, their futility, evolving and devolving in a background that was out of focus. And they wouldn't be able to fully remove themselves from human-based time and space. For a conscious mind needed to be part of the whole, like a rock was part of the whole unconsciously. And spending an eternity as a pine and spruce forest or the valley spirit that never died, without care or intention, convinced them only that pathology was power. And that was nothing new.

What was new was that these spirits went far beyond survival itself. They were outside of it. They suffered gloom, misery, exasperation, frustration, despair. They were suffering beyond death. This was what the church feared most. This was what it wanted to eliminate. Only through the repetition of lives could suffering be diminished. Things could only evolve because of death, and if there was no longer any death, that meant things were either no longer alive or else they were just undead. Just unlife.

The new priest often wondered whether insanity and godliness were the same creature. Was worshipping one insane god any more reasonable than worshipping people who'd been institutionalized? The church had always been an institution to measure one religious ecstasy against another—or one crackpot god against every other crackpot god.

Once, while the new priest was making his rounds, a blind and shrunken creature about to embark on its first day in the bardo cycle moaned in despair and muttered something incomprehensible before gasping hoarsely and bursting into tears.

"Enough." The new priest hated loud noises, especially of the sort coming from this tiny, feverish, infinitely aged figure lying on the ground with knees pulled up just below its chin and shaking in fear or pain or else in fear of pain.

The new priest wasn't incapable of human feelings, but the time would soon come when he'd have to give these up too. Already, he felt his emotions as dim shadows, too mild for his notice. They had become a second consciousness, a buried, intuitive layer below his postsentient mode of thought.

Witnessing another's human emotions, the new priest would feel his head ache the way it had in the period immediately after the operation in Exinia. He would feel as though his brain were being stabbed by a needle. His only nepenthe was the implanted memories, a vicious cure given to him by neurotechnicians during the operation itself—memories of the blackwood acacia trees that were said to still grow in the veldt of the Holy Land. The trees leaned with the wind, their bare boughs describing the ruins of the seasons.

The HAL was a lonely place. But there was a beauty to the desolation of surface dwelling, and when the day ran short of light, the night's stars looked like the swirling teeth of some unfathomable beast. During an ordinary day, the sky was bright blue and large over the plains; the stand of domes cast long shadows. The new priest was sheltered by those shadows and wove straw in them, to pass the time.

He was the keeper of the gate, that unmarked and undivinable entrance, a portal that couldn't be entered. That subterranean gate he remained with never opened, refusing to let anyone in or allow anything out. He didn't descend into the caverns of the empire and journey into the bowels of the labyrinth.

He'd never been there. No one else had, either. But it was more accurate to say that anyone who'd gone there couldn't return, that they were sealed inside the tomb world. The new priest knew that there were beings there, beings who were falling forever, at the event horizon, where time stopped. They'd made the choice to turn their world into a black hole: still alive when viewed from this world but already dead in their own.

Below this dungeon were the primordial figures whose bodily forms, awaiting the final transcendence, were only symbols. They constructed the HAL around them. These specimens were suspended in the middle of the city. These creatures of the vacuum, faceless postsentients, had their eyes and ears wired to sensors. They'd already passed through the event horizon into the singularity. They never ate. They never drank. They floated on the surfaces of black liquids that blasphemed and bubbled repugnant spheres capable of freeing nefarious forms. To see them was to know the only link between the tentacles of matter and thought.

Having abandoned and surpassed all form and all matter they had become Godlike, entering the blinding abyss of xenodivine darkness. Xeno-creaturality was joined with xeno-divinity to the point of vanishing. In this place there was neither beginning nor end. Neither here nor now. Neither one nor many. Neither before nor after.

The new priest's eyes sought only those who approached across the naked plains that stretched away to the end of the horizon, plains whitened by the bones of travellers.

The gigantic forms of the ten domes made musical sounds when the wind blew through their hollowed heads. At night they sounded like mournful creatures, and the sound was meant to signal to the pilgrims that they were near the city's entrance. The pilgrims grew shrill as the wind increased, and they swelled into a chorus. Their open mouths, each in a perpetual *O*, mimicked the distressing sound of the wind, again and again, which made it difficult to tell whether it was a pilgrimage or a funeral.

The sacrimentalizing of the ideal drug appealed to the souls who came to the domelike charnel houses. The urge for independence and self-determination and the urge for self-transcendence were fused with a third urge—the urge to worship by means of a coherent theology, something that was offered to those who came for the new priest's sabbatical treat.

It was no beatific vision. Animals were still obsessed with survival and human beings were still obsessed with words and notions. That religion would follow the ingestion of an ideal drug was also nothing new. The percept had merely swallowed the concept. Neither science nor superstition nor the logic behind a need captivated the pilgrims. What captivated them was simply appreciation for an intense beauty and a deeper significance. The new priest, going from dome to dome, thought this over many times.

Comprising a thicket of dark satin, the new priest's antlers were hollow like flutes. When he turned to the wind of the south, they issued a music of ineffable sweetness that drew all the ravished animals around him. Serpents twined about his legs. Wasps clustered in his nostrils. Birds settled on his antlers. But when he turned them toward the wind of the north, his antlers, thickly bristling, brought forth a sound of howling. Hideous and discordant cries proceeded from them. Forests startled with fear. Rivers reversed toward their sources. Husks of fruits burst open. Grasses stood erect.

When the wind wasn't blowing, the surface was silent, and that silence waged its own violence upon the new priest's self-contained state. There were, he thought, three types of silence central to the divine: the silence of the external world when one was alone; the silence of one's own inner thoughts when in prayer; and the enigmatic silence that came with being in the presence of God. But when all this failed, there was a final type of silence: the silence of bewilderment; the silence of the dumbfounded.

Above the subterranean city, he would contemplate the persistence of the corpses in the charnel houses, which gave him the strongest notion that death wasn't the end. And the new priest's state of contemplation was at its height and fullness when he was bewildered and dumbfounded by the silent corpses. The image of the corpses flowed through the conduit of his second brain, cleansing the doors of perception and bringing back only the most ego-dead, the most self-less, the most enlightened reports.

His second brain began to regress infinitely into the swirling shell of his drugged first brain. His mind was beyond itself, sliding subtly into its second mode of consciousness. As always, in this second state, he felt contempt for his former state. This was his true nemocentric vision of higher consciousness: the simulation of self as no one and nowhere. Because self only took him so far. He returned to thinking about his exegesis, which he composed there, impressing it directly into the grey matter that made it real.

There, at the top of the beacon, as he looked over the grassy plains through the eyes of the drug-god, he noticed that the drug's effect was proportional to distance. A perspective complicated by changes in spatial perception. The nearer something was, the more divinely other it became. The vast panorama before him, with view succeeding distant view, was hardly different from itself. By keeping this effect in mind, he could keep up with his mundane duties while still experiencing nirvana.

Falling from the tomb of Heaven was an incandescent light, an indifferent star plummeting to Earth. The huge, torched object hurtled through the cerulean depths of the planet's clear blue sky.

There was a reverberation as the land was struck by the brightness. The new priest didn't know if this was a product of his inner skies, caused by the drug, or something else.

The new priest no longer saw only grassland and woodland, an intoxicating green mosaic. The brightness was now in the field of yellowed oats and green wind-blown reeds that grew on the plains surrounding the beacon and its domes. The new priest, shifting from his second brain to his first, hastened to the spot. He had endured the excavation of his mind and was still recovering. Was his first brain now betraying him, or was it his second that was doing that?

When he came upon the brightness in the grass, he saw the edges of a sharp, golden light that emanated an unexpected coolness. Confused, he decided it was at least something like fire and so tried to put it out, but he couldn't affect it. This confused him all the more. He saw flames leaping, pulsating colours, and a horde of furiously fleeting shapes. What appeared to be burning was a piece of equipment. *Maybe a satellite*, the new priest thought. The brightness didn't seem to actually touch the grass. It was as if it couldn't reach it, as if its lines were the lines of some repelling force. After a time, the equipment stopped being so bright, and then it lost its brightness altogether. The equipment was cold, and he could see on its side the acronym *HAL*.

It was beyond the limits of his augmented senses to capture, beyond science and nonscience, but he believed that he was in the presence of some kind of organism. It was a transparent, ethereal being, catching and bending the light like a bead of quicksilver or a drop from a melting mirror—a spherical point warping in from four-dimensional space. Light refracted inside the sphere, and the organism inside was distorted, causing a visual break in the image of the organism.

Far above, the moon rolled unobscured down the western horizon. The pilgrims blinked through the gaping hole that was the main entrance to their domes. The other ecclesiastics looked through the high window cavities of the beacon and into the frozen light. The new priest looked as well, and slowly realized that something had changed.

The moon no longer held the unsettling glow. The tenting, which had protected it with its polymers from the vacuum of space, had gone dark.

The only thing still luminescent was the body of brightness curled up inside the equipment, a burning brightness of unmitigated reality. There was a cascade of sparks that the new priest somehow knew represented a living organism, but he couldn't prove it or disprove it.

At last, he could distinguish something like the appearance of a human body. It stared out through its own burning. A living torch burning the way a flower opens. Human geometry unfolded in a configuration of the dimensional divine. The shrouded jewel of the body shone with horrific intensity into the universe. He felt as if he were in the presence of a puzzle, a formless puzzle, in relation to which the materiality of his own body was but a garment of skin. The brightness spoke inexplicably, and then the fuzzy white phosphorescence went out. Its first contact was quickly followed by its last.

Only a haziness of the former brightness was left, as if it were obscuring itself through a glimmer that hinted at a still more impossible light, leaving nothing of its world behind but disbelief. And once the haze cleared completely, only thin, empty, metallic equipment remained.

The Blind Epilogue:
Desolation of Wrath

It remembered it had once believed that ecstasy was better than being God. It was wrong. Being God was much better. And so it had discarded humanity like an amniotic membrane discards a fetus. There was, after all, much more grandeur in the morose and rotting desolation of wrath. O sanctuary. O vengeance.

It still felt something for humanity, however, despite all the unstable chronicles of change. It didn't have a name for this feeling. But then, what they had between them never had a name.

Euronymous was the deformed image of the wrath of the Xenochrist. The heresiarch found itself in the sepulchre of the Xenochrist siege machine, at the locus of destruction, waiting for everything to be destroyed in one moment. The moment when everything would fall into lawlessness. It was revolting against everything and everybody.

A burst of whispers sounded through the dark space of the labyrinth, although the speakers remained unseen. The subvocalized voices themselves were invisible creatures floating in the inhuman darkness of the God machine. The swimming things had bodies only in a metaphoric sense. They appeared as postsentient mutations, living an embodied life beyond human consciousness. Monsters who no longer had any relation to the human.

What emerged on that day of gothic insurrection was a minor manifestation of its final form. It became a blasphemous apparition. Something resembling a face. It was an insinuation at first, composing itself of an image's shadow. A mirror-coloured thing. An incarnation of unverifiable fluidity accreting itself from its surroundings. Substancing unreality into a presence growing every moment more physical, more suited to realness. A harmony of abandonment and impulse, of unnatural and yet graceful postures, in that mystical language of limbs miraculously freed from the weight of corporeal matter, infused with new substantial form, as the breath of life. Miraculously transformed from the nothing that it was. Turned into image.

From the walls and floors came the syncopated thumping of myriad hearts. Euronymous had been hibernating for years in the metal coffin of a high-security isolation room whose limits it was ready to outgrow. The instant it realized that the moment of annihilation might finally come, it had locked itself up in the blackened hull of a spacecraft and launched itself into geosynchronous orbit. Euronymous, its body adrift, wouldn't be able to leave the vat it inhabited, or rather, that anomalous phenomena of rioting cells that the isolation tank contained, until everything had been destroyed.

It was here, holed up in this tomb floating through space, that Euronymous had ordered all the doors of the rooms to be closed. And the entrance to the modular space station itself was closed, and the courtyard, closed, and the fountain and garden, too, were closed. The execution of this tremendous task of thoroughly closing itself up inside the space habitat of the ecological cycling system, which Euronymous began to call the Astral Fortress, even though it was in fact a cryogenic storage facility, had been done so quietly, so peacefully, that it reminded Euronymous of the construction of Solomon's temple.

Metaphysically, this illusory closure closed on itself and left historical contingencies on the outside. Euronymous was in an unassailable place of both safety and shelter, at least at the moment. The place was locked up, bolted, and barred. This place that was never really built for people.

The Astral Fortress was in fact no longer a building at all, but a being, a distressed being that had, by degrees, become increasingly autonomous. And at times, these functionally autonomous parts even warred with one another, but never with Euronymous.

Enemies, Euronymous thought, with an instinctive, nonmammalian certainty, *are all there is to be found outside the Astral Fortress.*

There was actually no way to prevent someone outside from finding a way inside the Astral Fortress. It was, in fact, no use at all to build up the walls, so to speak, or install locks, or broaden the bars on the windows. Because in no previous period of history could a greater example of the principle of evil be expected. And acts of criminal violence occurred far more frequently at orbital properties than in the cities on Earth or in space.

Euronymous carried a weapon at all times. It was always reaching for the spiked club fastened to the back of its skeletal chair, the legs gilded bones. Euronymous had done it a hundred thousand times, for no reason at all but pure habit. It was absolutely unnecessary.

Under Euronymous's chair was spread a vulture's skin, and Euronymous was dressed in a damascene costume. It was in one of those rare but continuous absorptions. That is to say, Euronymous was reflecting, reflecting with dismay, in a state of pauseless dread—reflecting on the fact that Euronymous had never had anything whatsoever to give to God or even to give up for God's sake.

Euronymous was, after all, no longer even remotely human. It was no longer possible to distinguish meaningfully between its exobiological organism and the informational circuits in which its organism was enmeshed. And with a deadened gaze of glacial boredom, during those hours that felt like days or weeks or months or years or decades that dragged on at such humiliating length, Euronymous ferociously looked at sacred images, heard spiritual talks, and listened to religious music. Yet it was as if nothing had happened. In vain did Euronymous wait for God to take over and purge it in that renovation by fire that would be darkest for Euronymous and Euronymous alone. And now, it could neither retrace its steps nor expiate itself.

Euronymous prayed with the relics of heretics, with beads made of bones from the spine of a fish. Because the Xenochrist was on its way to be crucified again. In all its splendour and beauty and majesty, in all its holy courage and sacred suffering, summoning the dark powers of corporeal matter, in a flesh not flesh, just as Christ had been after his resurrection.

I am on my way to be crucified again, the Xenochrist was soon to say.

The inorganic Christ, cyborg figure of postsingularity humanity, would not only humanize data but computerized subjectivity.

The Xenochrist was expected to arrive unannounced, it being unbiblical to set an exact date, though every one of the signs of the second coming, that is to say, over twenty distinct signs of the Xenochrist's return, were in a state of fulfillment at the present moment.

The digital word of the Xenochrist couldn't fail. But Euronymous could.

The Xenochrist, when it came, came in all and for all, and each was a part of it. It was in the posthuman clades of life that sacked cities and countryside, and it was in unforeseen signs in the heavens whereby suddenly black rainbows, horns, and fires appeared.

Euronymous had neglected to prepare itself for the Xenochrist's return. But when Euronymous reflected on the fact that Judas had lived among the apostles, had been in continuous conversation with Christ himself and had been receiving direct transmission of the teachings, Euronymous realized that nothing was guaranteed. Euronymous was, however, singularly rich in every kind of morbidity and rottenness, and had a decidedly speculative, if not unquestionably mysterious, bond with the metaphysical. Because the dark side attracted Euronymous and mysticism got its feet off the ground. But total ecstasy didn't last very long and the other demons soon abandoned Euronymous.

The demons had duped Euronymous, and for its willingness to fall into the demons' beastly clutches, Euronymous had just as soon been abandoned. So that everywhere and always, obscene forms and fearful images rose before Euronymous. The demons would set traps into which Euronymous would walk and find itself hopelessly lost. It was coerced, if you will, into an aberrant eternity through an undying fixation on innocence. It happened over and over again, in its ongoing, naturally satanic existence. This or that demon would lure Euronymous into a trap, or several traps, thousands of traps even, and then desert Euronymous, leaving it all alone—alone in limitless despair because Euronymous felt drained of all its scandalous passions.

No one knew the least about this *unmensch*. Lost to time, Euronymous, the netherworld demon of rotting corpses, dwelled in the underworld. Only Euronymous's scandalous debauches of revolutionary demonology were known, the scandalous debauches that had led Euronymous here. And it was here, hidden at the end of time, awaiting the annihilation of the world, where no one was able to reach Euronymous—with no more constraints, with no more limits—that Euronymous had abandoned itself to those desolate plains, to that landscape of abomination, with its extinct craters yawning like the mouths of Sodom under a black sky. Here, only one tree grew, a tall pine that was an abnormally intense green colour. A sinister landscape in an equally sinister place.

And, again, here Euronymous was, on his elevated chair in a creepy, decaying industrial environment, somewhere between, in a strange bright dark. The whole interior of the Astral Fortress was blackened metal, studded with armoured orifices from floor to ceiling. Everything was black, inside and out.

And so, it was within this blackness where the wheel of Ixion, the wheel on which Euronymous had ceaselessly turned for so many long years, had stopped spinning, or at least slowed down considerably, so that it was only in the arms of Morpheus, in the deep splendours of those monstrous dreams. Here, in this blackness, Euronymous found the strength needed to make further sacrifices to its Venus.

Atrocious ritual crimes, villainous crimes, were an intimate thing for Euronymous, because it was in committing these crimes that Euronymous expressed something of its personality. It would demonstrate the plain structure of the relationship that, in the way of a natural disaster or a serial killer, might yet restore the connection between the Earth and humans.

Its whole being was predisposed to malefactions. It had razed to the ground villages and houses. It had burned churches after befouling the sacred images—after tearing tombstones from the altars, breaking the limbs off statues of the Virgin, looting the chalices and vessels and books, destroying the spires, shattering the bells, seizing all the possessions of the clergy.

But its previous sacrifices were overshadowed by the enormities of its latest sacrifice: the death, disappearance, and annihilation of everything that exists. And it was the skulls of these previous sacrifices that Euronymous sprinkled with the blood of his latest sacrifice, after it had eaten all the flesh off the corpses. But Euronymous was exhausted by the excesses of its debauchery and could go no further in this direction, in the destruction of value, because Euronymous had crossed the bounds of human infamy.

It all surged across its brain, all the blissful visions of enemies slain, every conceivable monstrosity, because this brain, its brain, now concentrated only on purging whatever might be passing through it. Because something was only clean if it no longer existed. And perhaps nothing existed. Because these unspeakable pleasures, these monstrous crimes, these abominable pastimes of torture, tears, terror, and blood, no longer satisfied Euronymous.

The human imagination has its limits, Euronymous thought. And if an infinity of love and goodness was attainable for some, the possibility of eternal evil still remained beyond its grasp.

There was no ascension into oblivion, where its spirit could roam free. For Euronymous had arrived at the gates of desolate eternity, having only come to feel something like an obsessive tenderness for those tortured subjects of its prolonged surveillance. Because the forces of oblivion were not only an enemy of love but an enemy of truth. Outside of both love and truth, all that Euronymous would leave behind was mere nothingness. All that Euronymous would do or ever could do: nothingness. Illusion alone was the only reality beneath the dilation of nothingness that was Euronymous, who already knew what brutal notion it was monotonously tormented by, to the point of madness: On Earth, God was nowhere to be found. Nothing but Satan existed on that satanic Earth. Only the emptiness of Satan existed. Earth was evil. Life on Earth was evil. There may have been life somewhere else ... but there wasn't.

Euronymous didn't even care that all imaginable earthly delights were piled up before it and would endure without end. It was nothing but disgusting garbage to it now. Total garbage. Euronymous knew that it was done for. And Euronymous had in fact come to take a certain satisfaction in feeling that it was done for, there being nothing else left to take satisfaction in.

Nothing lasts forever. Euronymous told itself from time to time that it had reached the end—several times a day, actually. It proclaimed that it didn't need to wait for the end in the midst of which it dwelled, for it itself dwelled in that ceaseless apocalypse. It only needed to recognize that it was already in the act of collapsing, and had been collapsing all along.

And now, at last, Euronymous thought, *I shall be free. Free of the rioting cells walled away behind surgical steel in this industrial life-support system. Free, forever, to inhabit an infinite horde of real bodies.*

And then the thing that Euronymous was moved with a terrible dignity. Moved to the next stage of its evolution.